Enchanted Thyme

Book One
The Delicious Adventure Series

by
Ariane Smith

recipes by Michael Wilson
illustrations by Andy Roth

Big Word Press - New York

www.enchantedthyme.com

Illustrations by Andy Roth
Cover illustration by Russell Lehman
Recipe illustrations by Felix Smith
Edited by Deborah Stark

Library of Congress Cataloging-in-Publication Data
Smith, Ariane.
Enchanted Thyme / by Ariane Smith ; with recipes by Michael Wilson and illustrations by Andy Roth.

p. cm.
Delicious adventure ; bk. 1

Summary: Peter and Belinda--children of a celebrity chef--venture deep into a forbidden forest, where they encounter magical creatures in their quest to find a meal to satisfy Queen Topstead, who has been cast under a horrible spell.

ISBN 978-0-9814872-0-5

1. Cooks—Juvenile fiction. 2. Gastronomy—Juvenile fiction. 3. Queens—Juvenile fiction. 4. Fairy tales. [1. Cooks—Fiction. 2. Gastronomy—Fiction. 3. Queens—Fiction. 4. Fairy tales.] I. Wilson, Michael, 1974- II. Roth, Andy. III. Title. IV. Series. Smith, Ariane. Delicious adventure ; bk. 1.

PZ7.S64285 En 2008
[Fic]—dc 22   2008921890

FIRST EDITION

10 9 8 7 6 5 4 3 2 1   08 09 10 11 12

Printed in the U.S.A.

Special Note to the Reader

I like to use big words, especially when they're part of a big adventure.
If you want to find out what some of them mean, check out our glossary which starts on page 113.

on page 113.

-The Author-

TO ALL WHO GENEROUSLY GAVE OF THEIR LOVE, GUIDANCE, EXPERTISE AND INSPIRATION

Abe Silverstein, Alison Naftal,
Alissa Mello, Anna Pop, Becky Geisel,
Bil Wright, Bill Haddad, Bob and Laura Yorburg,
Bruce Ditmas, Celeste Mulaney, Carol Cleveland,
Carolyn Roth, Celti and Rocco, Chris Phillips,
David Donovan, Deborah Stark, Endeavor Studios,
Diana Preisler, Diane Rooney, Elisabeth Carroll Smith,
Ernest Bradford Smith, Evan O'Neill,
Faith Bao, Felix Smith, Fiona Scoones, Frank Miata,
Grace Roth, Harriet Walsh Smith, Harry Lines,
HCCWG, The Hunterdon County Library, Ian Logan,
Ilana, Jake, and Jordyn Gelfand, Jack Stufflebeam,
Jeremy Glasser, Jim Sandner, Joel Roth, John Martin,
Karen Braga, Kristine Carter, Lainey Johns,
Laurie Edmunds, Lenora Bonéy, Linda Herring,
Lynette Stone, Marc Nohé, Margaret Dobbs, Mark McKenna,
Michael Kelly, Mike, Joy and Sammy DeFabrizio,
Nancy Bookchin, Patricia Burgess, Robert Malfi,
Robin Kornstein, Roslyn Stark, Ryan Compton,
Ryann Schachtel, Shannon Schachtel, Shela Xoregos,
Sheri Oshins, Suzanne Carroll, TPAC, Tim Weiler,
Tom Case, VLA

Table of Contents

Enchanted Thyme

Chapter One

There was once a time that was neither your time, my time, nor anyone else's. It was simply a moment unto itself. And, in this rare moment that seems to have magically slipped through our narrow concept of ticking clocks and calendars, exists the Kingdom of Enchanted Thyme. All those lucky enough to have had the great pleasure of visiting this fair land still speak of how it was the most beautiful, peaceful and delicious place imaginable. But that was then and this is now.

So begins our tale. It starts with two everyday children. I do say everyday because there is nothing particularly remarkable about them except, of course, to their father, Chef Michael. For you see, any good parent will attest to the fact that their children are extra-special, gifted, brilliant and most probably on their way to exceeding the heretofore measured levels of true genius. But, amongst themselves, Peter and Belinda are most happy to fit in with a normal crowd. In fact, at the tender ages of eight and ten respectively, being different is quite considered a handicap, something to carefully hide for fear that it might be indelicately pointed out by your peers, or, worse yet, those in the crowd to which you secretly wish to belong. So, like most of us, Peter and Belinda dedicated themselves to fitting in by having the "latest" -- the latest piece of shrunken technology, the latest inflatable gizmo-gadget flashing sport shoe, the latest word on the latest Hollywood pop icon, and most important to our two, the latest, greatest adventure story. In addition to all that, Peter and Belinda were lucky enough to have the coolest in status symbol commodities -- a chef for a parent. For this commodity has become "it" with the "in" crowd.

"Your dad cooks for you?" asked eleven-year-old Jennifer Rich, wide-eyed with disbelief as the school bus bumped down the road.

"Why of course," offered Belinda in her most grown-up manner answering one of the richest and most popular girls in school.

"He's a chef," added Belinda proudly.

"Professional," chimed in Peter who went on to add, "He makes us great stuff. And he always reads to us at bedtime."

Fearing Peter might be getting them into somewhat

uncool territory, Belinda quickly interjected, "What do your parents do?"

"Father owns a hedge fund and Mother stays home to take care of us," answered Jennifer rather bored.

"Oh, so your Mom makes you dinner, right?" asked Belinda trying to find some sort of common ground.

"And reads you stories and then puts you to bed?" added Peter, attempting to fit into the big girls' talk.

"No, nanny does that," answered Jennifer incredulously as she stared out the school bus window. "A chef, huh, like those guys on TV?" Jennifer continued sounding mildly interested.

"Not really," answered Belinda, but she was cut off by Peter's annoying enthusiasm.

"Dad makes us great stuff!" he repeated. "Last night we had macaroni with three gooey cheeses, sautéed broccoli, which it turns out I don't hate as much as I thought, and pirate's gold."

"Pirate's gold?" asked Jennifer with a smirk.

Realizing that he sounded like a bit of a dork, Peter quickly added, "But I like sushi, too."

Suddenly, there was silence punctuated by the gentle, lulling whirr of the near-empty bus as it continued its familiar rounds. Pulling up in front of the gated entrance to a very long hidden driveway, Jennifer popped up out of her seat and grabbed her bulging backpack.

"Bye," said Peter eagerly.

"Mm," was Jennifer's almost non-reply. Jennifer looked at Belinda for a second and said, "See ya," as she turned and bolted off the bus.

Her nanny stood there waiting by the driveway with Jennifer's two-year-old brother, Thaddeus. She thrust her backpack at the nanny, and all three turned to open the gate to the driveway.

"I kinda like her. She's nice," said Peter as he and Belinda started to get their things ready to get off at their stop.

"Oh, Peter," sighed Belinda shaking her head.

"What?"

"Nothing, I just wish we'd never moved." And with that, the bus ground to a halt. They clambered out in front of the bigger house Dad said had a better school system with bigger and better opportunities for them. They got up to the front door, and with Belinda's key, let themselves in.

Peter's
PIRATE'S GOLD

Serves 4

(Chef Michael, Peter and Belinda use organic ingredients whenever possible.)

2 lbs. Russet potatoes (about 4 medium potatoes), peeled and cut into chunks

2 ears of fresh yellow corn or one 14oz. can of nibblet corn, drained

1 Tablespoon olive oil

1 small onion, diced

2 large (or 4 small) carrots, peeled and sliced into penny-sized pieces

1 sprig of fresh thyme (optional)

1 Tablespoon butter

1/4 cup low-fat sour cream

1 cup warmed low-fat milk

1 pinch of salt (very small amount taken between your thumb and forefinger)

Pepper

- Place potatoes in medium pot and cover with cold water. Add a pinch of salt.

- Bring water to a boil, turn down and simmer until potatoes are soft (about 30-40 minutes).

While the potatoes are cooking...

- Shuck the ears of corn and rinse (if you're using fresh corn).

- Have an adult carefully cut the kernels off the cob.

- Drizzle the olive oil into a medium sauté pan.

- Sauté the onion first until it's clear, and then add the carrot slices.

- Turn down the heat, cover and cook for about 10 minutes, stirring occasionally.

- Add a touch of water if it begins to stick.

- Put the fresh or canned corn in with the carrots and onions and continue to simmer, covered, for 8 minutes.

- Add salt and pepper to taste.

- Taste the vegetables to see if they are slightly soft.

- Add the thyme and cook for 2 more minutes.
- Poke potatoes with fork (or sword) to check if they are done ...

... when done;

- Drain potatoes. Then return them to pot. Add butter.
- Mash with potato masher or sturdy whisk.
- Fold in sour cream and warm milk.
- Season with salt and pepper.
- Place corn and carrot mixture in the bottom of each serving bowl.
- Cover with mashed potatoes and serve.

NOW DIG THROUGH THE POTATOES TO FIND THE PIRATE'S GOLD AT THE BOTTOM AND DON'T FORGET TO EXCLAIM "AAAARGH!" AND "AHOY, MATE-Y!" WHILE YOU EAT IT.

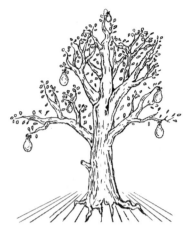

Chapter Two

*L*ater that night, during a rollicking game of "bed &
bounce," a game Peter swore he'd never give up and
Belinda swore she'd never admit to liking as much
as she did, their Dad, Michael, called from downstairs,
"Simmer down you two! Time for bed; it's getting late!"

"Yeeeeeeaaah!" shouted Peter as he took a giant leap off
the bed right into the pile of pillows he proudly dubbed
Mt. Rushmore. He landed with a *THUD*, and, without
skipping a beat, declared, "My turn to choose the story."

"You chose last time," objected Belinda as she began
resetting the pillows in anticipation of her spectacular
double jump with a half twisty motion.

"No way!" said Peter, not noticing how shrill his voice
had just gotten.

Belinda rushed over to strike an impenetrable stance

in front of the bookshelf. "Don't even think about it," she snarled, doing her best imitation of the cowgirl from a Wild West movie Dad had just taken them to.

"Pfffft," was Peter's dismissive retort as he pretended to mount a horse. With a twangy drawl he continued, "Now step aside, Ponchita, so's you don't get hurt."

But Belinda firmly stood her ground. With that challenge, Peter knew it was time to settle the score. He began by rushing the bookshelf while Belinda took great delight in body-blocking him. Finally, he decided that his foolproof dodge and weave technique would be the way to go. Unfortunately, that "way to go" turned out to be his pajama leg caught on the edge of the bed. Off he went, flying headlong into Belinda. They both hit the bookshelf full force. It toppled, sending volumes crashing down around them. No one was hurt, but through peals of laughter, Belinda managed to finally catch her breath and speak.

"Now look what you did!" she said assessing the damage.

"I did?" questioned Peter, "This was totally your fault!"

Cutting off the start of yet a new argument, Michael's voice boomed, "What's going on up there?" then he added more softly, "You two okay?"

"Yeah Dad," they both quickly replied.

"All right. Just hang tight. This is almost done. I'll be up in a minute."

Belinda stood up quickly. "C'mon, hurry! We gotta put

all these books back before Dad gets up here."

"Oh, all right," muttered Peter grudgingly, remembering how much he hated cleaning his room, and thinking how this was exactly the same. Instinctively, they formed an assembly line. Peter handed Belinda a book from the floor and, being taller, she placed it quickly on the bookshelf.

"C'mon, c'mon! Faster!" she commanded.

"Here," said Peter. But after a few minutes he began losing what little steam he had, so he slowly handed her an extra-huge stack. "Relax, will ya," he pleaded, now that there were only a few books left scattered on the floor. "We're almost done."

"'Bout time," snapped Belinda grabbing the books from him. He was about to respond to what he figured was a dig when the very last volume on the floor caught his attention.

"What was that?" asked Belinda. He didn't answer, but stood staring at the book. "It glowed," she pointed. "Red, I think. Did you see?" she asked tentatively. Still Peter didn't move. "Peter, say something."

It was an interminable split second before Peter was able to get out a *Shhhhhh* while still not moving a muscle. He then managed in a weak, raspy whisper, "We probably just thought we …", but before he could finish, again, the book glowed a bright eerie red, then stopped.

At that very same moment, the door to their bedroom flew open. Startled, Peter and Belinda turned to face the sudden intrusion. It was Dad.

"Whoa! Sorry. But I told you I was on my way up." He looked slightly perplexed at their pale, wide-eyed faces. He scanned the room suspiciously and then noticed the book lying on the floor. "Oh, great!" he said sounding truly pleased. "I see you managed to choose a book without the usual discourse." With that, he walked over and picked it up.

"*Enchanted Thyme*? I don't know this one. Is it from the library at school?" Neither Peter nor Belinda answered. "Hm." He started to read the back cover to see what it was about. "Okay, sounds good."

Peter at that point could contain himself no longer and blurted out, "We don't know where that came from. It just started to gl-" but before he could finish, Belinda's elbow jabbed him sharply in the ribs.

Peter winced as Belinda jumped in. "It might be a good idea to start reading from that ... I think," she said trying to sound convincing.

"Then we'd better get started. I still have hours of work to do tonight."

"What do you have to do?" asked Belinda as she and Peter slid into their beds.

"There's another magazine coming to do an article on the restaurant tomorrow and I have a lot to prepare."

Without waiting for a reply, Dad took his usual seat and cracked open the book. He looked up at them before starting and asked the all important, "You two brush your teeth?"

With a wide toothy grin they both shook their heads "yes."

"Good, now let's see. Chapter one." He cleared his throat, as usual, for a purely theatrical effect and continued, "Enchanted Thyme, Chapter One."

"You already said that," pointed out Belinda peevishly, eager to get into the story. "You're right," agreed Michael. "How 'bout this? Page one." This made Peter laugh, but he stopped when Belinda shot him a look.

Dad continued, "Long ago, in an old castle deep in the dark, thick forest of Enchanted Thyme, lived Queen Topstead. Her kingdom, which was once one of the richest in all the land, was now heavy under an evil curse cast by the Fricassee Fairy .

"Wait a second!" exclaimed Peter frowning.

"What's wrong Peter? You don't like this story?" asked Dad trying not to lose his patience at yet another interruption.

"Fricassee? I don't get what that means."

"Fricassee means to cut up and fry. It's a foodie reference. Get it?"

After a slight pause for reflection Peter said, "Got it."

"Good," snapped Belinda. "Now can we possibly get back to the story?"

"Sure," said Dad. After a small furtive sigh, he continued.

"In happier times, Queen Topstead's land was filled with vast orchards of silver trees that magically grew golden pears. Every evening, fairies were instructed by Queen Topstead to pick the fruit by moonlight, and by the first rays of dawn, leave a golden treasure under each of the poor villagers' pillows. Only the Fricassee Fairy refused to carry out the Queen's wishes, greedily hoarding the pears for herself. For this, she was banished from the kingdom."

Silently, two silver trees began to sprout behind Peter and Belinda's headboards.

They grew, and when they reached the ceiling and could grow no further, their branches arched over to hang gracefully above their beds. Each branch then proceeded to produce a shiny golden pear. No one noticed.

Dad continued the story, "To seek revenge, the Fricassee Fairy cast a horrible spell on the Queen. Now, no matter what the Queen ate, she would always be hungry."

Michael paused for a second to turn the page. Two golden pears from each of the silver trees growing in the bedroom secretly and gingerly dropped with a *plink* on Peter and Belinda's heads. They both immediately fell asleep. Having worked their magic, the two trees disappeared.

"I kinda like this story, don't you?" said Dad. His children didn't respond, for they were in a deep, dream-filled slumber. "Strange," thought Michael, since lights out had recently become such a struggle.

The Fairy's
Golden Pear Salad

Adorned with pomegranates and almonds

Serves 4

1 ripe pear, cored and sliced

¼ cup sliced almonds

½ of a pomegranate (or ½ cup red raspberries)

6 whole lettuce leaves such as Red Leaf or Green Leaf, Boston or Romaine

1 Tablespoon olive oil

1 teaspoon lemon juice

1/2 teaspoon honey

Salt

Pepper

1 large zip lock bag

- Place pear slices and almonds in zip lock bag and set aside.

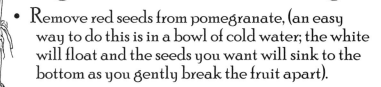

- Remove red seeds from pomegranate, (an easy way to do this is in a bowl of cold water; the white will float and the seeds you want will sink to the bottom as you gently break the fruit apart).

- Remove the red seeds from the water and add them to the bag with the pears and almonds, discarding the white part of the pomegranate.

- Tear 2 of the lettuce leaves into bite-sized pieces and also place in the bag.

- In a bowl, whisk together oil, lemon juice and honey to make dressing. Season with salt and pepper.

- Pour dressing into the bag. Seal and shake well.

- Take four whole lettuce leaves and arrange each one in four separate bowls. Evenly pour your salad into the center of each "leaf cup" and serve.

"NOTHING COMPARES TO A SWEET, GOLDEN PEAR."

~ QUOTH THE FAIRY

AS SHE WIPED THE JUICE FROM HER LIP.

Chapter Three

Michael closed the book and quietly placed it on the nightstand. He gently kissed his children's foreheads, and after pulling their blankets up to touch their chins, whispered, "Good night my sweet hellions."

He then tiptoed out of the room, mindful to keep the door slightly ajar as per Peter's old request. Going downstairs, distracted by thoughts of the very long night ahead, he missed the most unusual occurrence happening in his children's bedroom. For the book that Michael left on the nightstand in hopes that they would all somehow agree to continue it the following night, started to glow. Dimly at first and then with greater intensity. The red light grew so strong that the book's binding could not contain it. With a *whoosh* it popped open.

What swirled out was a funnel of glittery blue-green wind. It rushed from the open pages, and as the turbulence grew taller and wider, with a *pop,pop,pop* three furry orbs catapulted out of it. One hit the far corner of the ceiling. Another used its wings to stop gravity and then glide in a graceful arc, landing on Peter's blanketed foot. The third dramatically stopped itself and took center stage, the middle of Dad's reading chair. The three Royal Kitchen Mice -- Marjoram, Basil and Rosemary -- paused for a moment to take in their surroundings. After all, being sent on a mission is dangerous and even stealthy mice with wings can never be too careful.

For those of you who have ever met flying mice, these three were most unusual. Marjoram was the "toughie," a real no-nonsense urban mouse recruited from the Lower East Side. Before going into service for Queen Topstead and being granted her wings, she could be found "hangin' in the hood" sporty-like, "shootin' hoops." In contrast, when Rosemary was a little mouselette, she won a scholarship to the Mousery Ballet School, and hasn't taken off her pointe shoes or her tutu since. Then there was Basil, ah sweet Basil. He came from a long line of Shakespearean mousers. With a flourish of his cape he fancied himself a bit of a wordsmith. These champions were handpicked by the Queen herself for their extraordinary virtues: loyalty, bravery, strength and also because she found them downright cute. They, though, preferred to see themselves as renegade rodents with unflappable logic and penetrating insights.

They quickly set to work. Rosemary took a hold of Peter's blanketed big toe and gave it a good yank. Despite her delicate ballerina demeanor, she could pack a wallop.

"Ouch!" cried Peter as he bolted up to a sitting position.

"Huh?" mumbled Belinda half asleep.

Then Marjoram and Basil each grabbed one of Belinda's braids and gave a gentle tug.

"Peeeeeeee-teer!" whined Belinda groggily, convinced that he was up to one of his stupid practical jokes.

Peter, now fully awake, couldn't believe his eyes. No, it can't be. He must be dreaming. Two winged mice pulling on Belinda's braids? Impossible! "No more raiding the fridge before bedtime," he thought. "I knew I shouldn't have had that cold leftover macaroni with three gooey cheeses," he added. "But I love it!" he argued with himself. "No more!" he firmly stated out loud, this time hoping that such a strong declaration might return everything back to the way it was.

But he was about to find out that the way it was, would never be again ... ever.

Chef Michael's
Macaroni With 3 Gooey Cheeses

Serves 4-6

4 Tablespoons unsalted butter (1/2 stick)

6 Tablespoons unbleached flour

4 cups warm milk

1 teaspoon salt

1/2 teaspoon pepper

1 pinch nutmeg

3/4 cup shredded sharp cheddar cheese

3/4 cup shredded Monterey Jack cheese

3/4 cup shredded mozzarella cheese

1 lb. elbow macaroni (or your favorite shape)

- Melt butter in a large saucepan over medium heat.

- Add flour.

- Using a whisk, stir flour and butter together until smooth. Do not brown.

- Using a wooden spoon stir constantly, as you slowly add warm milk, 1 cup at a time. (Make sure mixture is smooth before adding each cup of milk.)

- Season with salt, pepper and nutmeg.

- Add half a cup of each cheese and remove from heat. Set aside.

- Fill large pot ¾ of the way with salted water and bring to a boil.

- Add macaroni and cook, stirring occasionally for 8-9 minutes.

- When macaroni is soft (not mushy) drain in colander.

- Put saucepan with the white sauce back on a low flame until warmed. Do not boil.

- Add macaroni, and stir well. Pour mixture into a greased 9x13 inch baking dish. Sprinkle remaining cheeses on top. Broil in oven until the cheese melts.

BON APPETIT, PETER!

Chapter Four

Basil and Marjoram's gentle tug on Belinda's braids was enough to wake her half way, but Peter's spoken declaration finished the job. She sprang out of bed and stood fully upright. As her eyes took focus, she had that weird split-second of not remembering exactly where she was. Then the room came clearly into view. There was her brother staring at her with his mouth agape.

"What are you doing?" asked Belinda, thinking that at that very moment he didn't look so swift. He kept staring. Finally, he slowly pointed to Belinda's head. Hovering on either side of it were Basil and Marjoram, each holding one of her braids straight out.

"What? … What?!" demanded Belinda, sure that Peter was just goofing on her. Any minute now he'd say "psych," then break into peals of laughter. She was sure of it.

But this time he didn't, and the frozen look on his face was beginning to get a bit spooky. Things didn't feel quite right, so Belinda walked over to the large mirror above her vanity. Now she could prove to herself that if this wasn't one of Peter's jokes, it was probably just the continuation of some crazy dream.

"Aha," she said to herself, noticing two mice fluttering as they each carried a braid suspended on either side of her head. "You see, a silly dream. Why, if I simply touch one of these, whatever they are, with my finger like this," which she got ready to do, "it will disappear." She then proceeded to poke Basil with her index finger, right on his backside.

Not expecting such a rude and uncalled for affront to his behind, Basil let out a very loud "squeeeek!", dropped Belinda's braid and went to hide in the bookshelf. Marjoram followed to make sure he was okay, leaving Rosemary to speak her mind, which she did in no uncertain terms.

"What a colossal bully!" she exclaimed as she stood on the tip of her pointe shoes while balancing on the edge of Peter's big toe. Being on pointe made her feel towering and important despite the fact that she was only about five inches tall. This small detail didn't matter when it came to valiantly protecting her friends. In her mind, she was an invincible giant.

Snapping out of his stupor, Peter let out a "yeee-oow-eee!" as he kicked his foot, dislodging Rosemary and sending her toppling down the side of the bed. *BOINK*! Her head hit the frame. *Whooosh*, her wings tangled in the dust ruffle and, *ker-plunk*, she landed ungracefully in a heap on the floor.

Meanwhile, Basil and Marjoram poked their heads out from either side of Belinda's secret diary. It was the one neither Dad nor Peter were allowed to touch. The one Aunt Irene gave her for her birthday. The one with the giant hidden padlock on the side of it. It was just the right shade of purple, and she loved it.

"Oh Peter!" cried Belinda horrified. "We scared them!"

"Whattayamean, scared *them*? Them what? What are them?" struggled Peter.

Ignoring this blathering, Belinda slowly tiptoed toward the bookshelf, but Basil and Marjoram once again darted behind her diary. So she tried to coax them out with a "tsk-tsk-tsk". That didn't work. She followed with, "Come out, we won't hurt you."

"Yeah right!" came Marjoram's booming reply as she stepped out with unexpected attitude. "Look what you just did!" she continued, pointing to Rosemary who was frantically trying to re-adjust her upside-down tutu and ruffled wings.

"Wow! They can talk!" gasped Peter in disbelief.

"Yeah-uh," replied Marjoram crossing her arms, dipping her hip and cocking her head, "But I trust you won't hold that against us." She paused, and then continued matter-of-factly, "See, it's like this. We did a little background check. Seems you two come up havin' da dish on da food. 'Cause a your Dad, our sources confirmed. Anyway, let me cut ta da scoopidy-doop: our Queen is messed up. Serious. And you two might just be da ones ta help." Peter and Belinda stared at each other in amazement. "You guys gettin' any a this?" They bobbed their heads in unison. "Oh, brother," sighed Marjoram shaking her head. "Basil m'mouse, could you help me out here?"

Slowly, from behind the diary peeked Basil. Making sure all was safe, he entered, waving his cape with a flourish. After a deep bow he addressed his new audience: "Master Peter. Mistress Belinda, we come here tonight, most des-per-ate of plight, hoping only that you lend us your ear. Our Queen, though once jolly, is consumed by dark folly. But we're told you might bring her good cheer."

"Huh?" gaped Peter, still stunned by what he was experiencing.

After smoothing her tutu, Rosemary decided to take things into her own paws. She flew right up to Peter and Belinda's faces. Logically, she began at the beginning,

"Our Queen is under a bad spell. The more she eats, the hungrier she gets. There's only one recipe that will satisfy her constant hunger. Everyone's topsy-turvy trying to figure out which recipe will work, but so far no one has succeeded. We think you two can help. Would you please consider coming back to the kingdom with us?"

"Peter and I?" asked Belinda skeptically. "We could probably get our Dad to help you."

"Far too big, wouldn't fit down da tunnel," interrupted Marjoram. "Besides, would we trust you with such an important mission if we thought you couldn't do it?"

After a second, a glimmer came to Belinda's eye. "The two of us? Really? Why, we'd love to go with you," she said with confidence, always ready for a good adventure.

"Belinda!" gasped Peter in horror. For you see, he was always up for reading about a good adventure but not necessarily going on one, especially one that might involve strange creatures, or far away lands, or scary monsters, or dark woods, or evil stepsisters, or a flesh-eating Cyclops, or two-headed beasts with flaming eyes and long sharp scaly …

"Peter? … Peter! Are you with us?" asked Belinda, noticing his blank stare.

"Me?" snapping back to attention with a gulp. "What makes you think I'm not with you?"

"You're not scared to go, are you?"

"Me? Scared? That's ridiculous! Of course not. It's just … well … we have school in the morning," he said, happy and smug with himself for finding an excuse.

"We'll have you home in plenty of time," assured Rosemary.

"Sure. But tomorrow morning I have a big presentation to do," argued Peter.

"What? Show 'n Tell?" quipped Marjoram sarcastically.

"No, certainly not," said Peter defending himself against such a babyish accusation. "I'm making a volcano. You know, papier maché and baking soda and …" as he continued to speak all eyes bore into him and his feeble excuse. "It's kinda cool. When you pour some seltzer in, stuff bubbles out the top …and I've been looking forward to …"

"Our entire kingdom is in grave jeopardy," interrupted Rosemary.

"The townsfolk are des-per-ate," added Basil.

"Our Queen may soon be a goner," said Marjoram sadly. "But that's all right. We understand. We were wrong, bothering you like this. C'mon guys, let's head back. Maybe if we're lucky we can find another solution before all is lost."

And, joined by Rosemary and Basil, Marjoram turned toward the book with sunken shoulders and droopy wings.

"Wait," said Peter. All three mice perked up and flew around his head.

"You mean you changed your mind?" asked Marjoram.

"I knew it!" glowed Rosemary while doing an extra graceful dip and swirl.

"To the castle we'll go! What ho!" proclaimed Basil.

"Yeah, what ho," said Peter unenthusiastically, knowing that at this point he couldn't possibly turn back.

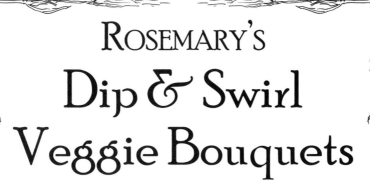

Rosemary's
Dip & Swirl Veggie Bouquets

Serves 4

For the veggies:

2 peeled carrots, cut into sticks

2 ribs of celery, cut into sticks

2 more ribs of celery, outer stalk peeled with a vegetable peeler from top to bottom to create 4 "ribbons"

1 red pepper, cored, seeded and cut into long, thin slices

½ lb. green beans, trimmed at the ends

2 Kirby cucumbers seeded and cut into strips

½ lb. sugar snap peas

- Rinse all the veggies in cold water. Then drain and set aside.

For the dip:

1¼ cups plain low-fat yogurt

½ cup fresh flat-leaf parsley, chopped

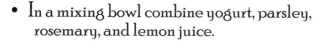

2 teaspoons fresh rosemary, chopped

1 Tablespoon lemon juice

Salt

Pepper

- In a mixing bowl combine yogurt, parsley, rosemary, and lemon juice.

- Mix well and season with salt and pepper to your liking.

- Divide dip into 4 separate dipping bowls and set aside.

To make the bouquets

- Alternating the vegetables for a colorful look, gather a few of each vegetable into what looks like a flower bouquet.

- Use a celery "ribbon" to tie up your bouquet.

- Now, using the dip, dip and swirl. Crunch, crunch, crunch a bunch!

- Try substituting the rosemary with thyme or basil or other fresh herbs in the dip.

SEE WHAT MAKES YOUR WINGS FLUTTER!

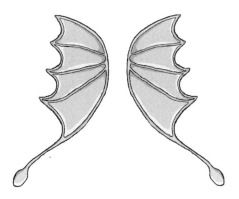

Chapter Five

How do we get there?" asked Belinda, so excited she felt like bursting. "Do we fly like you?" Just the mere thought of this had her jumping up and twirling like a mad ballerina.

"No, you can't fly by yourselves," said Rosemary.

"That's a relief," Peter sighed to himself.

"But don't worry. We can lift you up and transport you," continued Rosemary.

"Oh no!" said Peter flatly, "I'm not trusting a little bunch of meeses to fly me anywhere. No offense, of course." Pleased with himself for taking a strong stance, he paused. "You just point the way, and I'll walk. Both feet firmly touching the ground."

"It's 'at-a-way," motioned Marjoram toward the book.

"That-a-way?"

"Yup," nodded Marjoram.

"Good. I'll see you there." As Peter started off he was unaware that Basil and Marjoram had grabbed him by the back of his pajama top and were lifting him several feet off the ground. His legs continued a walking motion, but before long his body caught on to its sudden lack of gravity. "Hey!" exclaimed Peter, not sure what to make of his present condition. "You cut that out!"

This only made the mice more mischievous. Soon they began flying Peter all around the room. Despite his initial skepticism, he started to enjoy himself, leaving Belinda to jump up and down shouting, "What about me? Hey! Now me!!"

Rosemary grabbed the back of Belinda's PJs and soon she was whizzing around the room as well. This made Peter and Belinda quite giggly, which in turn made the mice quite giggly. But, as the mice's tittering squeaks grew more frequent, they began turning into deep guffaws. These were quite unexpectedly rude sounds from such small creatures.

Everyone's
Fizzly Wizzly and Most Dizzly Punch

Serves Lots!

12 ounces fresh or frozen raspberries

46 ounces pink lemonade

1 quart raspberry sherbet

2 liters ginger ale

- Place ½ of the raspberries (6 ounces) in a blender.

- Pour in enough pink lemonade to cover the raspberries and blend until smooth.

- Combine remaining pink lemonade, raspberries, blended mixture and sherbet in a festive punch bowl (or divide into 2 large pitchers).

- Stir until sherbet melts.

- Pour in ginger ale and serve.

MOST FIZZLY-WIZZLY!

Chapter Six

This jolly mayhem continued around and around the room, better than any amusement park ride they'd ever taken. Our two were so enthralled that they scarcely noticed the mice flying them in circles above the book like a pair of jumbo jets.

Suddenly, from the top of the high ceiling in their bedroom, the mice began a breakneck nose dive toward the night stand. As they quickly approached, Peter and Belinda began to realize what was happening. So they did what any two brave humans would do. They shut their eyes and held their breath in total fear. But, right before they were about to wildly crash into the book on their night stand, it popped open to allow a passageway through its pages. Surprisingly, this felt just like diving into the deep end of a swimming pool. There's always that moment of reckless abandon, the decision, followed by a plunge. Then all of a sudden you're in an unfamiliar world, murky, muffled, yet totally exhilarating.

Before they realized it, they were gliding down a glowing red tunnel. Further and further, "Perhaps to the center of the universe," thought Peter. For a while they floated past bright neon walls, which twisted and began transforming into a kaleidoscope of colors.

"Wow!" shouted Belinda to her brother. "These walls are psychedelic tie-dye! Too groovy!" she exclaimed.

Peter, not knowing what in the world she was talking about, didn't answer but pretended instead to be totally distracted by his surroundings.

As for Belinda, there was no other way to describe the tunnel except "groovy." For she had learned all about the word "groovy" from the time Dad took her shoe shopping.

When they got to the mall, he said, "For school you can have any pair you want as long as they're comfortable." This was great, since she had her heart set on a pair of white, chunky-healed go-go boots. All the older girls were wearing them. After getting her size and zipping them up, she noticed Dad's slight wince of disapproval.

"These are the ones you want?" he asked feebly. "No sneakers?" he added.

"I've got a closet full of those. I really want these. What's wrong, Dad? You don't like them?" she asked, knowing full well that he had told her she could have any pair she wanted.

"No, no it's not that. It's ... they're kind of groovy."

"Groovy?" asked Belinda, which launched Dad into a long-winded explanation of the word. He rambled on about the late 1960's, the peace movement, how everyone was so relaxed and the birth of tie-dye. He then went on about some band called The Beatles and started to sing one of their songs, which made Belinda really happy that none of her friends were around to witness this embarrassing grown-up moment.

Therefore, this tunnel struck her as groovy and fun. Unfortunately, to Peter it was kind of frightening. As they dropped further and further, he began to worry about where they might end up.

"Are we going all the way to the earth's core? It could be very hot there," fretted Peter. Thinking about this made his body feel heavy and molten. As if to match his mood, the walls of the tunnel began to melt.

Without notice, they hit bottom.

"Ouch! That smarts," cried Peter, rubbing his behind.

"No time to rest," urged Marjoram, "We gotta go. See that door?" She pointed ahead to an old wooden door with rusty hinges, peeling black paint and a bright red apple for a doorknob. "That's the way to ..."

But before she could finish, Peter interjected, "Where?"

Without answering, the mice flew up to a little window at the top of the door. It had tiny green shutters shaped like leaves. They knocked several times before the shutters flew open and nothing but a large, bulbous nose poked through.

"Yeee-ah-es?" asked a wheezy, high-pitched voice that continued, "Who's there?"

The mice replied in unison, "Fiddle-dee-bop-ee. Fiddle-dee-boop-ee. We're the ones that work with you-pee."

There was a slight pause, followed by some muttering from behind the door. "We really do need to re-think those passwords," complained the voice of the nose as it retreated.

Abruptly, the shutters closed and the door opened with a *creeeeek*. The nose clumsily scuttled away on two stringy legs, disappearing into the underbrush.

"What was that?!" exclaimed Peter.

"That? Why that's the knows-it-all nose from nowhere," answered Rosemary.

"Oh. Sure. Well, where'd he go?" he muttered nervously.

"Nowhere."

What lay before them was absolute darkness. They could see almost nothing. Not wanting to enter, but not wishing to be left behind, Peter and Belinda followed the mice as they scampered through the door.

A blast of cold wind blew dense fog, which curled around their feet. As their eyes struggled to adjust, the old black door slammed behind them with a thunderous, *boom*!

Slowly, faint shadows became ghostly outlines. Trees, gnarled and bent, took shape. It was a forest cloaked in eerie silence. This silence was broken by the occasional "*Caw*" from a flock of sinister-looking ravens as they began swooping from tree to tree.

They hadn't taken but a few steps when a family of humongous beetles scuttled right in front of Peter. "Aaah!" he yelled, having never seen a bug that was bigger than his skateboard.

"Don't worry; they don't bite," said Rosemary reassuringly.

"Oh, right," said Peter feeling slightly stupid and still very apprehensive.

"Yeah, they're nothin'. Wait 'til you get a load a' Creepy," quipped Marjoram.

"Creepy?" gulped Peter as he tried to look toward his sister to see if she was as frightened as he was. But much to his annoyance, she had walked on ahead and seemed to be totally enjoying herself. She bent down to pet one of the shiny black bugs. The beetle stopped to rub the back of her hand with its antennae. Smiling, she got up and started skipping around with a sudden burst of increased enthusiasm. This was even more annoying to Peter.

Belinda's
Groovy Grapes
and other green fruit
Salad

Serves 4

2 cups seedless green grapes

1 honeydew melon

2 kiwi fruits

1 green Granny Smith apple

$\frac{1}{2}$ lime

$\frac{1}{2}$ cup sparkling white grape juice

- Remove stems from grapes.

- Cut melon in half, and remove seeds and rind;
  then dice into bite-sized pieces.

- Peel kiwi and chop into quarters.

- Core apple and thinly slice.

- Place apple slices in a bowl with the grapes, honeydew and kiwi.

- Squeeze the lime juice over fruit and toss.

- Chill for one hour.

- When ready to serve, scoop into individual bowls and pour sparkling grape juice on top.

TOO GROOVY!

Chapter Seven

Are we here? Is this the way to your kingdom? Where's the castle? When do we get to meet the Queen?" asked Belinda without waiting for any answers.

Ssshhhh, the mice warned with squinched looks on their faces.

"We hafta be quiet, careful and stick together," instructed Marjoram.

"Careful?" gulped Peter. "Okay, but why?" he asked, not really wanting to know.

"A great monster-beast lurks about the Forbidden Forest," said Basil as his eyes darted to and fro. "And alas, our wings don't work in the Forbidden Forest," he continued, lifting one of his wings and watching it fall back in a droop.

"Monster-beast?" repeated Peter.

"Creepy. 'Tis the Fricassee Fairy's pet," responded Basil.

"Cree-py?" asked Peter, his voice sticking and his eyes wide with fear. Just then, a rather large black raven landed on a tree branch directly above them. Peter let out a startled "Whoa!" while ducking his head into his shoulders.

"Don't worry, dude," said Marjoram "you'll have plenty a notice when Creepy's comin' around."

"Yeah?" said Peter trying to regain his composure. He wished once again that he had never agreed to this adventure and that since he had, sort of, he could at least be holding his sister's hand right now. But that might seem a little too babyish.

"Sure," continued Marjoram, "There's nothin' ta be scared of. You'll be able ta hear him slither along da forest floor. Right, Basil?"

Basil, whose attention was focused on keeping track of Belinda and Rosemary as they walked ahead, nodded distractedly, "Oh my word, yes. What's more, his eyes glow like embers in the dark. That beast-y is a good eighty-six feet long. Inky. And shiny with blue-black scales and tremendous claws."

"Don't forget that jaw fulla razor-sharp teeth." added Marjoram.

"Indeed," agreed Basil, "one definitely knows when the monster-beast is lurking about."

"So you see, there's absolutely no reason ta be worried," shrugged Marjoram.

With that, Basil and Marjoram went on to join Belinda

and Rosemary, leaving Peter a few steps behind to ponder the situation. This was fine, until a twig snapped behind him and he dangerously catapulted forward trying to catch up to everyone else. Now all together, they ventured deeper into the Forbidden Forest, Creepy or no Creepy.

The Forbidden Forest's
Black Raven Bog
with Vanilla Fog

Serves about 6

½ cup granulated sugar

½ teaspoon pure vanilla extract

2 eggs

1⅛ cup heavy cream

1 cup milk

1 Tablespoon unsweetened cocoa powder

½ loaf pre~sliced, white bread cut into ½ inch cubes

2 ounces semi~sweet chocolate or carob chips

3 ripe bananas peeled and cut into small pieces

1½ cups vanilla or maple flavored yogurt

• Preheat oven to 350.

- In a bowl, whisk together sugar, vanilla, eggs, cream, milk and cocoa powder.

- Add bread cubes and toss.

- Add chocolate or carob and bananas to bread mixture and toss.

- Spray a 8 x 4 ½ x 2 ½ inch loaf pan with cooking spray to coat.

- Fill with bread mixture.

- Bake uncovered 1 hour and 15 minutes until top is slightly crisp.

- Allow the "bog" to cool slightly and firm up in the pan.

- Remove from pan and cut into slices.

- Serve warm with vanilla or maple flavored yogurt drizzled on top.

"CAW CAW!" THIS RECIPE GETS RAVENLY REVIEWS!

Chapter Eight

Forging on, the group came upon a pathway lined with huge umbrellas. No, wait. These weren't umbrellas at all, they were giant mushrooms. Toadstools, to be exact. The infamous fairy tale red caps all covered with white polka dots. Seeing gigantic poisonous mushrooms was impressive enough, but when the mice touched their caps, they lit up.

This was so unexpected that Peter and Belinda both uttered, "Awesome!"

As they walked down the toadstool-lined path, each step they took illuminated a new mushroom up above and on either side of them.

"They're so cool," said Peter enthusiastically, forgetting for a moment about potential monsters, school, or the fact that he wasn't at home tucked into his nice, warm bed.

They walked on for a while in silence, each person or mouse lost in thought. Basil mused that after this the Queen would be so pleased with him she'd hold a grand celebration in his honor. That coveted bronze medal placed around his neck would definitely complement his cranberry-velvet cape.

Rosemary thought that if this mission were successful, she'd choreograph a new ballet in the Queen's honor and call it "Tripoltnik."

Marjoram kept focused on the task at hand, but every once in a while imagined herself shooting baskets with a fly pair of new sneakers. These of course, would have eighteen-karat gold shoelaces. "Sah-weet," she thought to herself.

Peter and Belinda, on the other hand, had thoughts too numerous to mention.

Everyone continued walking since the mice still couldn't use their wings.

Soon, the path grew steeper. Peter and Belinda found themselves climbing over bigger and bigger obstacles. What started out as small white rocks became large white boulders that had a strange, spiky surface. Missing her footing, Belinda stumbled backward, only to discover that the "rocks" were actually as light as a feather.

"What are these things?" she asked the mice.

"Bread crumbs," answered Rosemary matter-of-factly.

"Seasoned with fresh Italian herbs," added Basil.

"Try one," encouraged Marjoram. "They're savory, not sweet."

"I've never seen bread crumbs this big," said Peter as he reluctantly ripped a piece off one and popped it in his mouth. "Mmmmmm," he murmured, not realizing until now how hungry he was. Belinda followed his example, and soon they were both stuffing their faces with tender chunks of crunchy, savory bread.

"Delicious, right?" asked Rosemary. They both shook their heads "yes" having more than once been reminded by Dad not to talk with their mouths full.

"Please don't eat too many. Orgoglio uses them to find his way home," requested Rosemary.

"Orgoglio? Who's that?" managed Peter before taking another huge bite.

"The resident giant, of course," said Marjoram, adding, "Now, c'mon."

Suddenly, the bread that had just been so moist and delicious stuck like sandpaper to the back of Peter and Belinda's throats. Still, they were able to follow the mice as they navigated the steep incline.

Upward the mice clambered as they quickly reached the top of what seemed to have become a mountain. Peter and Belinda tried to keep pace but soon realized that they had lost track of the mice.

"Basil! Marjoram!!" called Peter followed by Belinda's even louder, "Rose-ma-reee!?!"

Three furry faces with pointy noses poked out from up above them with a simultaneous, "*Shhhh*! He's still sleeping!"

Peter and Belinda squinted hard to make out the "he" that was supposed to still be sleeping. Seeing nothing, they turned to each other with a shrug.

Then, out of nowhere, two rolls of thick rope came bounding down the mountain, unraveling along the way. The end of each rope landed in front of Peter and Belinda's feet.

"C'mon up," whispered Marjoram.

"Quietly and quickly," added Rosemary.

"Make assurance double sure, but with haste," declared Basil before the other two mice could cut him off with, "We just said that."

"Indeed," was Basil's somewhat deflated reply.

Belinda grabbed the rope and dug her feet into the surprisingly squishy brown cliff. Peter copied her and soon all their strenuous jungle gym days seemed to pay off. Up the steep side they scaled, hand over hand, foot by foot with super acrobatic skill.

Feeling like Olympic gold medalists when they finally reached the top, they jumped forward with arms raised and shouted "Ta-da!" All at once the ground beneath them began to rumble and shake.

"Oh dear," was all Rosemary could manage before the ground heaved straight up, sending everyone tumbling. Just in the nick of time, they were each able to grab a piece of rope to cling to for dear life.

Dangling to and fro, Peter and Belinda looked up to see

a huge face looking down at them. Orgoglio stared for a minute at the tiny beings hanging on the strings of his lace-up shirt. For the mountain they had been climbing was in fact, the stomach of a sleeping giant.

"Fee, fie," rumbled the giant before stopping abruptly. "D' I say Foe already?" he added innocently.

"No Orgoglio, you didn't," screamed Marjoram as she struggled not to loose her grip.

"Oh, right. Now where was I?" he asked slowly.

"Fum …Fum Orgoglio," answered Marjoram trying her best not to sound impatient.

"Oh, yeah, Fum. Well, you guys already know the rest. Didn't eat too many a me bread crumbs, I hope," he said as his eyes narrowed into button holes. "Need um ta get meself home," he continued.

"Plenty left," offered Rosemary quickly.

"Good. Right then. Where you all a goin'?" he asked.

"To the Kingdom," yelled Basil whose tired hold on the shirt string made him even more anxious to get going.

"Oh, right. Well then, let me help you," answered Orgoglio as he scooped everyone up in his hand. "Got ta get you ta safety, eh? No runnin' inta Creepy or the Fairy, eh? Don't know which-a one's the worser, I'll tell you that much." Everyone nodded in agreement. He stopped short, "Hold on then. Who are these two?" asked Orgoglio eyeballing Peter and Belinda.

"They're our new friends," said Rosemary.

"Humans," added Basil proudly.

"Humans? Aaaaahhhh," screamed Orgoglio who went on, "Don't like humans!! Talk too much and never know what they're talkin' 'bout!! I's never liked 'em."

He was about to drop everyone when Rosemary intervened. "These two are different, Orgoglio. We assure you. They've come to help the Queen. We need them. They've traveled such a long way, Orgoglio. Be kind to them."

"Kindness," boomed the giant's reverberating voice. "That's what you want, eh?" His head tilted and then looked away as he considered the idea. He turned back. "They're supposed to help 'er highness?" he asked, and then with the utmost tenderness added, "cause I love Queen Topstead. Do anything ta help 'er."

Marjoram quickly jumped in with, "Copy that. 'S why we're here! We know you can help us get to Fairy's End."

"Oh sure. Fairy's End; that's where the Fricassee Fairy can't go no further. I sure know where that is. Watch." And with that, Orgoglio, stretching out the hand that held everyone, swept it gracefully to the side. From the palm of his cupped hand, everyone stood on their tippy-toes to peer over his fingers.

The land below resembled a patchwork quilt. The view was spectacular. Lush, green broccoli-shaped treetops surrounded ponds that resembled small, rain-filled footprints.

Seeing their enjoyment, Orgoglio decided to show off. He dipped his hand down low and then zigzagged it up over his head. Peter and Belinda's grinning, wind-blown faces encouraged him to be even more reckless. He brushed the tops of trees and then in one fell swoop skimmed a pond, causing the water to splash up in a tall spray. Everyone squealed with drenched delight.

Not unlike a small kid in a big bathtub who sometimes forgets to scrub up, Orgoglio lost track of his main mission. Yet his playfulness was infectious, so much so that no one except Rosemary noticed the dark apparition that had begun to follow them.

Orgoglio's
Giant Croutons

8 cups (approximately 8 slices) of your favorite hearty bread (for example: whole grain, french, peasant, etc.), torn into bite-sized pieces

1/2 teaspoon garlic powder

1/4 cup olive oil

6 Tablespoons grated Parmesan cheese

- Preheat oven to 350.

- Place bread and garlic powder in a large mixing bowl.

- Drizzle with olive oil.

- Toss well.

- Sprinkle with cheese and toss again.

- Spread bread pieces onto a large baking sheet in a single layer.

- Bake until golden brown for 10 to 15 minutes, moving bread around occasionally.

- Cool before eating.

Store croutons in an airtight container for up to 1 week.

SAVE SOME FOR FINDING YOUR WAY HOME AS WELL AS FOR YUMMY SWAMP STEW (SEE PAGE 59).

Chapter Nine

W hat was that?" thought Rosemary as the others still squealed with delight at every spin and drop. She thought she saw a slight flicker out of the corner of her eye, but when she looked, nothing was there. Perhaps it might have been a shadow of something that quickly darted behind a tree? Or was it the waning moon playing tricks? Finally, the presence was unmistakable. Smoldering eyes pierced through foggy branches, glowing, burning bright with fire and with hatred.

"Orgoglio!" she screamed, her voice shrill with alarm. "Please get us to Fairy's End. Quickly!" was all she could offer as explanation, for she was trying not to fathom what a horrible fate would await them if they were caught by the Fricassee Fairy.

It was said that a few unlucky folk had been crunched

like carrot sticks in the jaws of her pet, Creepy. Others, the Fricassee Fairy had seasoned, rolled in flour and deep-fried. One tragic traveler simply died of fright. There seemed to be a great number of stories about the Fricassee Fairy, each one more ghastly than the last. But one thing was certain: her anger had festered over the years and caused her to become quite hideous.

Of the mice, Orgoglio knew Rosemary to be the most levelheaded. Hearing her panic was unusual, so he was sure something was very wrong.

He cupped both hands protectively around his friends and stood to his full height. This brought him head and shoulders way above the clouds. He took a step forward, which caused the ground beneath him to shake.

Then he whispered into his cupped hands, "I'll have you there in no ti ...," but before he could finish, *ZAP*, a fiery lightening bolt shot out and hit his left knuckle. It burned a deep hole where it landed, but Orgoglio didn't stop or remove his protective hand cover. Instead, he took another step forward only to be punished with an even more powerful bolt of lightening from the Fricassee Fairy.

This one hit the thin, back part of his ankle. The sting was so excruciating that he bit his lip and closed his eyes, wincing for a split second. But Orgoglio had triumphed. With only two giant steps, there they were, right in front of Fairy's End. He was proud of himself. Despite the pain, he had won.

Opening his cupped hands carefully, he was relieved to see his friends alive and well. He gently lowered them to the first of five smooth stepping stones leading to a tall iron gate all covered with ivy. These stones rose out of the murky black swamp that forever bubbled and swirled in front of Fairy's End.

With his free hand, Orgoglio reached over to open the gate.

That's when Belinda noticed the deep wound. "Orgoglio, you're hurt! We've got to take care of you."

Quickly pulling his hand back and covering it with his shirtsleeve, Orgoglio feigned a crooked smile. "Oh that, miss; it's nothin'. A scratch. Now you all go on. You've got 'ta hurry. Go on now. Go!!"

At his urging, one by one they jumped to the next shiny black stone. Each one turned to look back. Once more he had to urge them forward, and only with great reluctance did they continue on. Rosemary led the way while Basil valiantly stayed a step or two behind to watch their backs. With each one helping the next, they carefully jumped from stone to stone. Finally, upon reaching the last one, they turned to wave good-bye. With a smile and a wink, the loveable giant lumbered into the woods.

That's when the stone on which they were standing began to violently shift. Losing their balance and almost falling into the swampy waters below, they clung to each other.

Rosemary, the first to regain her footing, nimbly jumped through the open gate. She then turned and extended her paw to help steady Peter, who leaped through with no problem. After this brave jump however, his knees wobbled with fear and nearly buckled beneath him.

Next was Marjoram, who helped Belinda through just as the stone began to rise and fall violently.

Basil was left balancing as best he could when *SNAP*, out of nowhere a huge set of gleaming, razor-sharp teeth narrowly missed him. This stone was alive. Worse, it was connected to a huge mouth with monstrous fangs. For the stone, shiny and black, wasn't a stone at all but the back of the great monster-beast. Yes, it was the dreaded Creepy.

Creepy had been peacefully sleeping in the cool, swampy ooze. Now he was totally awake and wasn't the least bit happy about the whole situation. His eyes locked on Basil. Basil froze. Creepy's reptilian head rose up from his long neck and remained deadly still. His pupils narrowed, his nostrils flared and the slight darting of a forked, blood-red tongue thrust itself into Basil's face.

Instantly, Basil regained his composure. Finding his wits, he went bolting toward the gate, but something snapped him back. One of Creepy's claws had grasped his cape. Basil's attempt at forward motion created a reverse slingshot. He fell, belly up, right in the middle of Creepy's back.

Thinking quickly, Peter grabbed a nearby broken tree branch, jumped back through the gate and used it to try and dislodge Basil from the monster's grasp. The branch was just long enough to reach over and barely skim the top of the cape. His first attempt was futile. Creepy's claw wouldn't budge. The second try had Peter balancing on one leg in order to get the branch even closer.

At this same moment, Creepy began to rise up even more. He *swooshed* back and snapped again at Basil, but this only succeeded in ripping the cape in two, sending both Peter and Basil tumbling down the monster's back. *SPLOOF!* The two brave fellows unwittingly landed in the swampy mud, right in front of the great monster-beast.

Creepy's eyes glared at Peter and Basil lying helpless below him. He smacked his lips in anticipation of a juicy, protein-filled snack. As his serpent-like mouth opened and drew back, a single, frothy white pearl of saliva glistened and rolled down the front of his fangs. It dangled for a moment and then hung before Basil and Peter's horrified faces. He was ready to pounce.

The frightful jaws drew back even further when out of nowhere, Orgoglio's foot forcefully stomped on the creature's long tail. Creepy let out a blood-curdling *screech*, followed by a vicious *hiss*.

A moment of painful silence allowed Peter and Basil a split second to scramble out of the ooze and run toward the open gate of Fairy's End. As they approached, *ZAP*, a bolt of fiery lightening flew past them singeing the delicate hair on Basil's left ear. *ZING!* Another bolt flew between Peter and Belinda, searing a hole in the ivy growing on the gate.

"C'mon!" screamed Belinda as she grabbed Peter's hand

and Basil's paw, pulling them through with all her might. Now safe, they all turned back to their great friend, Orgoglio, who had returned just in the nick of time.

But he was far too occupied to see them. For high above his head he was holding Creepy by the tail and swinging him 'round and 'round like a pinwheel as the giant gates of Fairy's End began to close.

Creepy's
Swamp Stew

Serves 4

1 15-ounce can of white beans, drained and rinsed

1 Tablespoon olive oil

1 Tablespoon chopped garlic

1/3 cup diced carrots

1/3 cup sliced celery

1/3 cup Spanish or yellow onions

2 cups of your favorite mixed fresh vegetables such as corn, mushrooms, zucchini, yellow squash, broccoli or red peppers, diced

1 32-ounce can or carton of vegetable stock or broth

1 sprig fresh thyme

1 bay leaf

Salt

Pepper

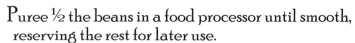

- Puree ½ the beans in a food processor until smooth, reserving the rest for later use.

- In a medium pot, over low heat, cook garlic in olive oil until golden brown (about 30 seconds).

- Add carrot, celery, onion and cook until onions are clear (3-4 minutes).

- Add all remaining vegetables, the whole beans and stock.

- Turn up the heat and add thyme and bay leaf. Simmer 15 - 20 minutes until vegetables are softened. Remove the thyme and bay leaf.

- Add bean puree, season with salt and pepper; then simmer 5 minutes more.

- Serve in bowls with Orgoglio's Giant Croutons. (See page 40).

BUBBLE, BUBBLE,
SWAMP OF TROUBLE.

Chapter Ten

Just as they passed through the gate at Fairy's End, it closed with a resounding, *k-klang*!

"Open the gate, we have to help Orgoglio!" cried Belinda.

"There's nothing we can do. The gate is already closed," said Rosemary. As a tear came to Belinda's eye, the mice gently urged her forward. "Don't worry; he'll be fine. And, we have more work to do."

On they went. The Forbidden Forest was now far behind them. Gone was the air of gloom and doom.

Here, a brilliant sun illuminated row after row of silver trees dotted with golden pears. The shimmer was so intense that at first they had to squint in order to see anything.

Vast orchards spread across rolling fields to the foot of a steep mountain. Occasionally, a cloud floated in front of the glimmering sun. This allowed Peter and Belinda the momentary glimpse of a large, far-away castle peeking through mist.

"C'mon, Peter!" cried Belinda. "Look! We're here! And it looks just like I thought it would," she beamed, "like in the book."

Off she went running up the mountain. Her enthusiasm propelled her far ahead of everyone else. The mice didn't try to stop her, for they knew she was safe here.

Belinda raced up to one of the silver trees and tenderly plucked a small golden pear off of its bottom branch. Turning back to everyone, she proudly exclaimed, "For Dad!" after which she thrust it safely into her pocket.

They continued through the sun-dappled orchards and up the mountain, getting closer and closer to the castle. As they approached, Peter and Belinda noticed two odd-looking men dressed in shades of plum. These militaristic visions in purple were stationed on either side of a drawbridge. Frowning under ridiculous horned, magenta-colored hats, they both drew lavender swords and pointed them at the mice.

"Who goes there?" demanded Gustavo, the guard on the left.

Marjoram rolled her eyes and answered, "It's us, da Royal Kitchen Mice. We're back from fulfillin' our mission."

"Oh yes. Of course," replied Gustavo as he pointed to his mate. "Rudolfo needs glasses. He didn't recognize you again. You may pass." Both guards bowed with a flourish.

"Gee thanks," muttered Marjoram flatly as they crossed the drawbridge leading up to the castle.

Behind them, they heard Rudolfo seething at Gustavo. "Why'd you say that? I don't need glasses!"

To which Gustavo replied, "But you must admit they couldn't hurt. They'd make you look smart."

This enraged Rudolfo even more, as he began to really raise his voice, "*You* make a simple mistake and yet you always find some sort of stupid way to blame it on *me*. Well, that's just not going to work anymore…"

"Work? Work you say?!! Well that's odd that you should know what that word means since it's been ages since you've done any."

"Oh, yeah?"

"Yeah!!!"

As the guards' lively debate escalated, Peter, Belinda and the mice entered the castle, thus hearing only the following momentary utterances: "Why you, SNIPPITTY SNAPPITY and FOO-FLUFFITY BLAPPITY!"

"Oh yeah?!!"

"Yeah! And what's more, double yeah!!!!" Their angry voices finally trailed off as everyone went farther into the cold, dim castle. Not a sound could be heard.

"Where is everybody?" asked Peter loudly, not expecting the booming echo that bounced back "… body, body, body," before faintly trailing off into the darkness. Just for fun Peter and Belinda tried out loud "hellos" that answered them back threefold from far away nooks and crannies. As this novelty began to wear off, they were left silently following the mice through a low, crooked doorway and then down a steep, spiral staircase. One by one they wound their way. Round and round. It seemed endless.

"Sheesh," said Peter to emphasize how tired of this he was growing. "Where are we going? The dungeon?" he asked in a smart-alecky way, not expecting a "yes" from all three Mice.

"Oh, now that really does it," he said shaking his head and turning around to go back up the stairs. "I am soooo outta here!" But as he turned, everyone jumped to grab hold of his still damp and swampy pajamas.

"Oh, no," exclaimed Rosemary, "we would never take you to the dungeon, silly. We just pass it along the way to the Royal Kitchen," she explained.

"Oh," said Peter. "I figured that. I mean I knew there was nothing to be afraid of down here, right?"

"Certainly not," replied Basil emphatically.

"None of the typical ogres, or wizards, or witches, or stuff like that, right?"

"Actually …" started Rosemary before she was cut off by Marjoram's, "Nah, nothin' crazy like that."

"No giant talking green gargoyles, right?" continued Peter.

"Well …" all three mice said hesitantly. They looked at each other for a moment before Rosemary quickly said,

"Funny you should mention gargoyles."

"Yeah, funny," added Marjoram tilting her head and squinting her eyes at Peter with a "How did you guess?" look.

Basil took over with, "'Tis a great noble creature. Gentle, trustworthy …"

"Kinda big," interjected Marjoram as Basil and Rosemary shot her a dirty look. "Well, he is," she said defending herself. "His name is Gothel," she continued.

"Gothel?" repeated Belinda nervously, "What a cool-o name!" she said with unconvincing enthusiasm, attempting to distract her brother from the fact that there was probably some sort of gigantic gargoyle monster lurking about the dark underbelly of this castle. Peter didn't reply, but frowned at his sister as he began to reluctantly follow the mice back down the winding staircase.

As they went on, Peter started to get a little mad at himself. He was sort of tired of being scared. Maybe, he thought, he should try making the best of things. That's what Dad would say.

When they reached the bottom step, Peter actually started to think about what a great adventure this was. He would be able to brag about it at school. He began to feel brave and proud of himself. He didn't even flinch when they passed a dungeon on the way to the Royal Kitchen. He decided that all the skeletons hanging in shackles from the wall probably weren't even real. And that rat scuttling about the damp floor darting in and out of the straw-strewn cells was made out of plastic, with wheels on the bottom. It was just like in a Hollywood movie. This was a run-of-the-mill, make-believe set. The more he thought this, the straighter, stronger and faster he became. Soon he was way in the lead as they headed toward the Royal Kitchen.

As our motley crew of mice, boy and girl approached their destination, these few quiet moments were broken by a plate whizzing dangerously past their heads. It crashed into the wall, narrowly missing Peter's head. *THUD*! *THUD*! Two pots hit the same spot, and, *TANG*, a pan followed close behind. Belinda grabbed her brother as they both ducked down to avoid the drinking glass that wildly shattered above them.

Then the loud scolding of a very deep voice could be heard. "No. No. And again I say no! … You call this a ROYAL dish? I call it garbage. It doesn't work. You haven't got it right, for I'm still hungry. HUN-GREEEEE!! Do you HEAR ME?" concluded the thunderous voice as several large oil paintings rattled off the wall and fell down in splinters. The voice continued, "There must be some way to break this blasted spell. You're simply not trying hard enough." No one answered or moved for a moment.

Then a dull, shuffling sound rose from the kitchen. This was accompanied by a "Yes, your Majesty. Certainly, dear Sovereign. Absolutely, your Grace," repeated over and over in a sing-song fashion. It was underscored by a *shuffle, shuffle, scrape; shuffle, shuffle, scrape.* The sound grew louder as a huddle of white jackets and checkered pants came bowing, shuffling and muttering backwards from the kitchen. They were a rather odd sight with their stop-start motion. Just as the clump of chefs was almost completely out of the kitchen, a hefty platter whizzed through the crowd, cutting it in two. They scattered as it crashed against the far wall and fell into a million shards.

Queen Topstead's bellowing started again; only this time it was even louder. "Make sure you don't come back until you've solved the riddle to that blasted spell and made a dish that will finally satisfy me. Chefs you call yourselves! Hah! Why I've never seen such a sorry bunch of rotten bananas. DO YOU HEAR ME?!!"

Like a magnet, they drew themselves immediately back into a clump and started tiptoeing backward muttering, "Yes, your Highness. Of course, my Queen. Quite right your ..." That's when Peter and Belinda saw the Queen's large shadow looming as it approached the kitchen door.

"She must be at least seven feet tall," he whispered to his sister.

"You're not kidding. Bigger than Orgoglio."

As she approached the door, her shadow grew taller and taller. The footsteps grew louder and louder, as everyone's eyes grew wider and wider. Even Belinda was truly scared. Then, this most ominous presence passed through the doorway. Finally they were able to lay eyes on the fearsome

Queen. There she was, and she was …three feet tall?! With a really BIG mouth! The small but imposing figure wore a dress of royal blue taffeta stitched with silver thread. Her headpiece looked like an upside-down crescent moon. It was adorned with a shear gold cloth that fell in a long train behind her. She glared at her group of chefs.

"Well?" she asked forcefully. "Oh, stop quivering!!" she screamed at the top of her lungs. This only made the chefs look more pitiful and shake even more. She continued, "I've seen Hasty Puddings have more backbone. Or should I say, jelly doughnuts? Hmmmm …" She paused for a moment looking somewhat befuddled. "Jelly doughnuts don't have backbones, but then again, neither do Hasty Puddings. So what in tarnation does that blasted saying stand for?! I mean how 'bout making Hasty-Jelly-Pudding-Doughnuts? And putting a backbone in each one? Then both sayings would be right. Hmmm. Well, I think that might be the solution."

"To what my Queen?" asked the very smallest chef meekly.

"Oh, isn't it obvious? Do I have to spell everything out?" She paused, glaring at them. "I demand hasty doughnut jelly puddings without backbones. But be sure to make some with."

This left everyone speechless. Finally, a brave soul from the very back spoke up. "With what?" quivered the voice.

"Backbones, you idiot!!" screamed the Queen who then

picked up the nearest coffee pot and hurled it at them. "I can't believe this!" she went on, "and what's more, I'm hungry. AGAIN!! A-GAAAAAAAIIINNN!"

As the final syllable in her rant finished, Rosemary whispered to Peter and Belinda, "The Queen's a bit grumpy today."

To which Marjoram added, "More like everyday, these days."

And, Basil jumped in with, "Therefore, 'tis good measure, for the Queen's pleasure, we brought you hither. Now let us not dither."

"Huh?" asked Peter still not quite connecting the dots.

So Belinda took over, "Basil means it's a good thing that they brought us here. We can try to help find the recipe that will break the Fricassee Fairy's spell. If we do, after the Queen eats it, she'll stop being hungry and mean all the time. She'll be satisfied. Am I right?" She turned to the mice.

"Absolutely," beamed Rosemary.

"Indubitably," added Basil.

"Cool beans," quipped Marjoram, giving Belinda and a reluctant Peter, a high five.

Meanwhile, the pitiful clump of chefs continued to shuffle about. When the Queen clapped her hands, they scattered like pin balls in a mad dash to fulfill her wishes.

Her focus quickly shifted to her Royal Kitchen Mice, who were now peeking out from behind Belinda's braids. "Back from your sojourn, I see." she said sternly before breaking into a wide smile that completely changed the shape of her face. "Tell me it was successful. Be the beacon of light in my presently dreary existence." She stopped and sighed, pondering for a moment. Her index finger found its way up to her chin, which she nervously began to tap. "Or should I say, ray of light. Now I'm not quite sure. Ray? Beacon? Or, I suppose one could mean angel. Yes, I like that. Angels. You do, after all have wings. So ..." She paused for a moment, taking a deep breath in order to fuel another long-winded debate with herself.

Marjoram seized the opportunity to bravely interrupt, "Your Highness," she began, "our most noble Queen, we present to you, Peter and Belinda."

Basil added, "They're descendants of a very famous chef."

"We're what?" blurted Peter.

Shhhh, whispered Marjoram who went on, "Don't blow it. If she likes you, come wintertime, you'll still have something between your shoulders ta hang a hat on."

"You don't mean?" asked Belinda, for the first time showing serious concern, "off with your ... you-know-what?!"

The mice didn't rush to answer her, so Peter naïvely asked, "What?"

To which all the mice shot back, "Head!!!"

A gulp was Peter's only reply as he and Belinda stood dumbfounded and speechless.

"Well don't just stand there gulping!" shouted the Queen,

who then went on as gently as she could muster. "Come forward and let's have a look at you."

For a second, no one budged, so Rosemary gently pushed Belinda toward the Queen and whispered, "Bow and curtsy." Even frightened, Belinda was able to do this with beautiful aplomb. Basil then gave Peter a small shove forward. He stiffly bowed in front of the Queen.

Softly as she could, Queen Topstead declared, "I welcome you to my Kingdom. Well actually, it's more of a Queendom. The King was ..." But before she could go off on another tangent, she caught herself and instead asked, "Tell me why you've decided to come here? From the looks of you, it's likely been a long and very frightening trip."

Unprompted, Peter bravely answered, "We've come here to help you and the Kingdom ... I mean, Queendom."

Charmed, the Queen softened even more and turned to the mice. "You've told them all about my unfortunate circumstances?"

"Yes, my Queen," they answered in unison.

"Good. Then we are all free to move on. Let us proceed to the very heart of this castle," she beamed, "my Royal Kitchen." She then nimbly *swooshed* off in that direction.

Queen Topstead's
Hasty-Tasty
Pudding
(with or without backbones)

Serves 4-6

1/2 cup long grain white rice

1/2 cup sugar

1 Tablespoon unsalted butter

1 teaspoon pure vanilla extract

1 small cinnamon stick (backbone)

4 cups milk

1 pinch salt

1 egg

1/2 cup light cream

Ground cinnamon

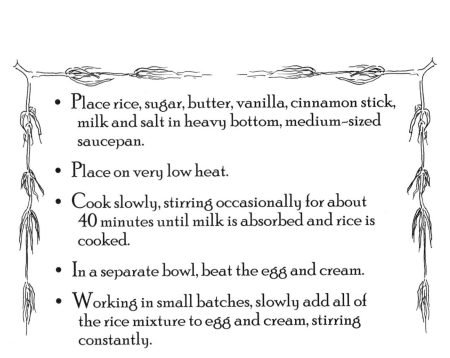

- Place rice, sugar, butter, vanilla, cinnamon stick, milk and salt in heavy bottom, medium-sized saucepan.

- Place on very low heat.

- Cook slowly, stirring occasionally for about 40 minutes until milk is absorbed and rice is cooked.

- In a separate bowl, beat the egg and cream.

- Working in small batches, slowly add all of the rice mixture to egg and cream, stirring constantly.

- After removing and discarding the cinnamon stick (backbone), pour mixture into shallow, 9x12 dish.

- Cover with plastic wrap, push wrap directly on top of rice in order to avoid drying it out.

- Refrigerate for two hours.

- When ready to serve, scoop into bowls and top with a light sprinkle of ground cinnamon.

YOU CAN ALWAYS ADD YOUR FAVORITE DRIED FRUIT OR NUTS. RAISINS, APRICOTS, CHERRIES, WALNUTS OR ALMONDS ARE ALWAYS TASTY AND NOT SO HASTY! ... UNLESS, OF COURSE, YOU'RE THE QUEEN.

Chapter Eleven

My incredible strength alone will tucker out this great monster-beasty," thought Orgoglio boastfully as he continued to twirl Creepy high above the Forbidden Forest.

As the giant's twirling movements began to pick up a certain rhythm, his large hips went swinging about to and fro. Soon he was humming a merry little tune. The Mexican Hat Dance, to be exact. Each "ta-dum, ta-dum, ta-dum," was punctuated with a "cha-cha," by banging poor Creepy's head on a nearby surface. It fascinated Orgoglio that by using a tree, a rock, or the top of a mountain he was able to create different sounds. The poor beast felt nothing more than a growing annoyance, but Orgoglio once again started having so much fun that he forgot about his main mission. Or, for that matter, that Creepy's fangs might do him a great deal of harm.

Now our dancing giant moved from Mexican rhythms to a more frenetic Salsa. He was twirling, hip-bumping and humming with dizzying speed. These moves were all quite graceful for a big-hearted but lumbering giant. He waived Creepy all about the forest in a "cha-cha-cha" and a "cha-cha-ting".

He started to make up some really great steps when all of a sudden his foot hit an unexpected pothole, a forgotten swimming pool once used by the Fricassee Fairy. Abandoned long ago, it was now filled with algae and dead leaves. The pool was a sad remnant from when the fairy was still happy and in Queen Topstead's good graces.

His ankle twisted painfully and his whole leg gave out beneath him. He landed with the same deafening *thud* as a falling tree. Unhurt, Creepy landed alongside him and seized the opportunity to lunge at Orgoglio. He plunged his teeth into the nearest protruding part of the giant, his buttocks, also known as the fanny, behind, tushie, bottom, tuchus, rear end, gluteus maximus, and derriére. Whatever you call it, one thing is for sure, getting bitten there by a monster-beast is far from a pleasant experience.

"Yeeeeoooowzzzaaa!" wailed Orgoglio, stars appearing before his eyes.

Orgoglio's
Dancing Salsa
with Pineapple, Mango and Tomatoes
Yields 4 cups ... Serves Lots!

$1/2$ pineapple, peeled, cored and diced into small pieces

1 ripe mango, peeled and diced into small pieces

$1\frac{1}{2}$ cups diced, ripe tomatoes

$1/2$ can drained and rinsed black beans

1 red pepper, finely diced

2 scallions, thinly sliced

1 Tablespoon lime juice

2 Tablespoons olive oil

Salt

Pepper

- Combine all ingredients in a large mixing bowl.

- Season with salt and pepper.

- Enjoy with your favorite tortilla chips, pita chips, or dancing Giant.

CHA~CHA~TING!

Chapter Twelve

Everyone scrambled to keep up with Queen Topstead as she scurried toward the Royal Kitchen. Her little legs moved like lightening as they sped past what remained of the neglected ballrooms, waiting chambers and symphony halls to the only room that she now cared about.

Upon entering, Belinda and Peter were awestruck. Gleaming copper pots and pans hung hither and thither from the ceiling. The kitchen was equipped with every cooking gizmo-gadget ever invented. Rows of gleaming marble countertops showcased mixers, dicers, dough hooks and designer rolling pins. Separating them were Below-Freezing refrigerators, Hades stoves and Wishy-Washy dishwashers.

"Jeez," said Peter. "Dad would love this."

"Yeah," Belinda sighed wistfully, wishing for a moment

that Dad was with them.

The only thing missing from this dream kitchen was a chef. Or a sous-chef. Or even a busboy. There was an odd silence to the whole place. They went on, through room after room. Then from somewhere up ahead, came a slight clanging sound. As they followed along, the sound grew stronger and stronger. With it, came a flickering glow.

Finally, in what seemed to be the very last room, they came upon the back of a white-jacketed chef who was gently closing the door of an enormous red oven. At that same moment, Peter's elbow accidentally brushed several cans stacked on the counter behind them. *Bing! Bang*! The cans crashed to the floor.

"Oh, Mon Dieu!" the chef exclaimed as he spun around to face them. "Sacré la table et le crayon! My soufflé! She will be ruined!"

When Peter and Belinda finally had a chance to see his face, they couldn't believe their eyes. This chef looked exactly like their Dad. Only Dad was wearing a big black moustache waxed to a thin curlicue at each end. Strange. And if it was Dad, they each thought, why was he speaking with a heavy French accent? They squinted at him. He squinted back.

Finally, Belinda said, "Dad?" But before he could answer, smoke started billowing out of the big red oven. Jerking around, he flung open the oven door and pulled out his ill-fated soufflé. It was completely flat and totally burnt.

"Oh, la-la, la-la, la-la!" he exclaimed almost on the verge of tears as he used a kitchen rag to fan great clouds of billowing smoke. "C'est ruined," he lamented. "Once again I will have failed to solve zee riddle. I shall never be named zee top chef in Queen Scene Magazine. I will not ever make zee right dish to save zee Queen. I can't even ..." But before he could finish, he began sobbing, big mournful sobs.

Not quite knowing what to say, no one said anything. After a short while his sobs dwindled to a sniffle. He raised his head and looked around. Seeing Queen Topstead, he immediately pulled himself together and took a full bow.

The Queen turned to Peter and Belinda, "This is our head chef. Chef Michelle Mon-Shoo Shablee Poo-Boo."

"At your servees," he replied, once again bowing.

"We call him Chef M for simplicity," she added smiling. "He is our most gifted and brilliant chef. But alas, he has yet to find a dish that will satisfy me. Try as he may. That is why I am truly happy you are here." She motioned toward Peter and Belinda, "Chef M, I present to you two new sous-chefs. A little idea the mice cooked up to help you. I hope they live up to their reputations. By all joining forces, you should be able to whip up something delicious. Dinner is precisely in ..." she looked at the hour glass on her wrist, scrutinizing it, "two hours. And fair warning," she leaned in closer, dropping any semblance of a smile, "I'm not only hungry, but VORACIOUS! See you then."

Queen Topstead turned and darted out of the kitchen

leaving Chef M with his two new wards. He immediately began fretting, "Oooh-la-la this", and "Oooh-la-la that." All the while he was pacing frantically back and forth.

No one could get his attention until the mice flew in front of his face asking, "How can we help you?"

Shrugging, he replied, "I am all out of ideas. Je suis finis! N'est pas?" This must have meant something bad in French, because Chef M looked like he was once more on the verge of tears.

Rosemary calmly offered, "Why not call on the Magic Mushroom?"

He pondered the suggestion a split second and then his face lit up. "I forgot all about him!"

The mice rallied together and flew over to one of the large, flat tiles that made up the kitchen floor. It looked just like all the others only this one had a round wrought iron pull attached to its' edge. The mice grabbed hold of the pull and yanked it with all their might. The heavy slab didn't budge. They tried again. The third time they were joined by Peter and Belinda, but to no avail.

Just as they were losing hope, *frooooom*, a panel in the ceiling opened and a scaly-green arm with a large claw came down. A single, sharp nail from the claw grabbed the round pull and drew the stone back with ease. The artichoke-looking appendage then retreated back into the ceiling.

"Thanks Gothel," cried the mice as the arm disappeared.

"That was Gothel?" asked Belinda.

"Yeah, he likes ta hang out in da refrigerators or in da castle's super-secret passageways," replied Marjoram as she started to lift a black-lacquered box out of the opening in the kitchen floor.

"There are secret passageways in here?" asked Peter surveying the walls.

"Lots," answered the mice, to which he surprisingly muttered, "Cool."

But before he could ponder any kind of behind-the-wall adventure, the mice had gathered around the box and were about to knock on its lid. That's when Chef M rushed over, pushing them aside.

He began, "Oh Magic Mushroom! We summon zee to help us wiz zees terrible curse. You, who are full of zee weezdom. You, who are always on zee ball. You, who are full of zee…"

"Baloney!" cried the Magic Mushroom as the box's lid flew open and up he popped. He was sporting a bushy, brown moustache and looked somewhat like a portobello mushroom with big buggy eyes. He was a quite comical fellow, even more so because he took himself quite seriously.

"Oy!" he blurted, "enough already with what I am full of. Greatness, no doubt. Either that or baloney. I prefer the latter. Burp! … 'Scuse me. Never touch the stuff. But let's not lose track of the fact that you've come to see me because you've got some sort of problem. How do I know, you ask?" he shrugged his shoulders. "Easy. No one ever comes to inquire if the Magic Mushroom is available to have lunch. Or to say, 'Magic Mushroom, let's take in a movie, something fun.' No, it's always, 'Oh, Magic Mushroom can you do this for me.' Or, 'Magic Mushroom, tell me the meaning of that.' Brother! And here I am, sitting in the dark all day long. That's okay, I'm used to it. Don't trouble yourself about me. Really. I'll just sit here ... in the dark ... all alone ... no really. I'm fine ... but now that you should bring it up, would it hurt anyone to once in a while come by and..."

"Magic Mushroom," interrupted Marjoram "you like livin' in da dark. That's your thing, dude."

"Don't change the subject," snapped the Magic Mushroom, "and what's more, if you don't mind, could we get on with things? I happen to be very busy today."

Having no idea what to do with his apparently crusty bad mood, no one spoke. But Rosemary quickly broke the silence with, "We don't know what we should serve to Queen Topstead."

"Yeah, everyone here is fresh outta any clue," added Marjoram.

"Farklempt?" asked the Magic Mushroom, his ego finally swayed by the fact that he might be instrumental in helping them.

"What does "farklempt" mean?" whispered Peter.

"We'll tell you later," whispered Rosemary.

"All right then," declared the Magic Mushroom, "let's get down to business." He ducked into his black lacquered box and re-emerged wearing a big, lime-green turban which had an iridescent blue gem smack in the middle, surrounded by a burst of peacock feathers. He looked so absolutely ridiculous that Peter and Belinda tried really hard not to laugh. This involved not looking at each other.

Suddenly, the Magic Mushroom got very still. His eyes started to spin around in his head. His bushy, brown moustache began to twitch. Rings of smoke puffed and curled out from under the turban. Then he began making a faint "Hmmmmmmmm" sound. As the sound grew louder it tickled the front of his moustache and then billowed out in a "Hmmmmmmmmmmm-ooooy. Hmmmmmmmmmmm-ooooy. Hmmmmmmmmmmm-ooooy." Melodically he added, "Ga-zing-a, ga-zong-a, ga-zoo." He repeated this chant several times. Then his eyes rolled back into his head. They closed and he went into an even deeper trance.

"What's he doing?" whispered Peter.

Shhhhhh, cautioned Marjoram, who added, "we just gotta let him do his stuff."

"Oh," nodded Peter, clearly at a loss over what "his stuff" could possibly be.

After a breathless silence, the Magic Mushroom's eyes burst open and rolled around and around in their sockets. The blue gem in his turban lit up and began flashing the words "Tilt, Tilt, Tilt." He resembled a Las Vegas slot machine. Then his mouth popped open. His tongue rolled out, and there at the tip was a tiny folded piece of white paper. Chef M reached over and grabbed the paper.

Bowing gratefully, he said, "Merci bien, Monsieur Magic Mushroom."

"No problem," he replied tartly. "I live to serve. Now would you please close my lid? After all that, I'm exhausted."

"Oh sure," said Peter, happy to oblige. He quickly shut the lid. *HONK!* The tip of the Magic Mushroom's nose caught as it closed.

"Oy!" exclaimed the Magic Mushroom, who continued, "Could you try to be a bit more careful?"

"Sorry," said Peter hoping he hadn't hurt the grumpy little fellow.

"Don't worry, that happens all the time. We keep hinting that he's gotten a little rounder and might need a bigger box, but he keeps insisting he doesn't," whispered Rosemary.

"So what's on the piece of paper?" asked Belinda excitedly.

"It's another riddle," answered Marjoram.

"C'mon, let's read it," said Peter with surprising eagerness.

"Voila, here it eez," pronounced Chef M as he handed the bit of paper to Basil. "Sweet Basil, with your beautiful voice, would you do zee honors?"

"Delighted," glowed Basil, always more than happy to show off his mellifluous voice. With one paw he theatrically swirled his cape while simultaneously bowing his head. He then unfolded the little slip of paper and began with gusto:

I THRIVE IN SAND, ROUND AND LUE.
PLUCKED FROM A USH, I COME TO YOU.
IN SPRING YOU TASTE ME
SWEET AND TART.
UT NOW YOU'LL FIND ME
IF YOU'RE SMART.

When Basil finished reading, there was a pause. All three mice looked at each other, not quite sure what to make of the verse. Basil rubbed his nose. Marjoram tapped her foot while Rosemary smoothed and re-smoothed the top of her tutu. Chef M paced back and forth with great agitation. Only Peter and Belinda seemed to have a plan.

The Magic Mushroom's
Las Vegas Lunch

Serves 4

1 can solid white tuna packed in water

1/2 rib of celery, chopped fine

2-3 Tablespoons light mayo, depending on how moist
you like it to be

1 Tablespoon lemon juice

Salt

Pepper

4 slices of avocado (optional)

2 baby carrots, cut into thin strips (optional)

4 large whole lettuce leaves (Red Leaf, Green Leaf or
Boston work best)

- Open can of tuna and press out as much of the liquid
  as possible.

- Place tuna in a bowl with celery, mayo, and lemon
  juice.

- Season with salt and pepper.
- Blend well.
- Place lettuce leaves on four individual plates.
- Place equal amounts of tuna into each leaf.
- Top with avocado or carrot if you wish.
- Fold in sides of lettuce and then roll closed with tuna inside.

PICK UP AND ENJOY, MAKING SURE YOU EXCLAIM THINGS LIKE, "OY! HOW DELISH!"

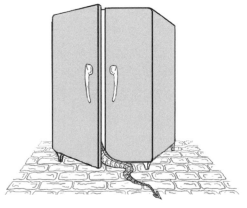

Chapter Thirteen

B elinda and Peter picked a quiet spot to study the little poem. After all, it might hold the key to the secret recipe. Their conference lasted through several rounds of head shaking, hand gesturing, whispering and, finally, when the dust settled, Peter exclaimed, "We've got it! We solved the riddle."

"You did?" beamed Rosemary, so excited her wings began to flutter uncontrollably.

"Yeah. Before each of the weird words that don't make sense, put the letter *b*. Then read it and see if the whole riddle doesn't make more sense," urged Peter. The mice and Chef M gathered around Peter and Belinda to try out their theory.

Chef M was the first to exclaim, "Eureka! 'Zay have it right!"

"See?" said Belinda, "now it makes sense," and she read aloud:

I THRIVE IN SAND, ROUND AND BLUE.
PLUCKED FROM A BUSH, I COME TO YOU.
IN SPRING YOU TASTE ME
SWEET AND TART.
BUT NOW YOU'LL FIND ME IF YOU'RE
SMART.

"Don't you get it? It's talking about …" But, before she could finish Chef M interjected, "Blueberries!"

"Right!" added Peter. "I'll bet we can make an awesome blueberry dish to satisfy the Queen."

"Oh, no, no, no, no, no!" cried Chef M. "Impossible!"

"Why?" was everyone's response.

"Because zay are out of season. Fini. No more. There is not one to be found in all zee land. Oh, la-la!" He shook his head dejectedly, "We are un-done."

Chef M was almost on the verge of tears when the mice flew up to him. "Don't worry. We'll all help," assured Rosemary.

"Yeah, no problem," added Marjoram.

"Most certainly," chimed in Basil, though for once he looked kind of skeptical.

Breaking the brief gloomy silence, Belinda exclaimed, "Hey! I've got an idea. Let's think-tank this problem."

"Yeah, that'll work," agreed Peter enthusiastically.

"Think what?" was the response from everyone else.

"Dad does that with us when we're trying to find a solution to something that seems impossible. We toss out ideas and he writes them down. Then we go back through them and pick the best one," explained Belinda as Chef M's face brightened a bit. "I'll start," she continued. "We could go to a nearby Queendom and borrow some blueberries."

"Yeah! Great idea. I'll bet New Jersey has tons!" added Peter.

"Peter, that's not a King or Queendom, that's a state," corrected Belinda.

"So what? I happen to know they grow lots of blueberries there."

"How far is it?" interrupted Rosemary, being her usual practical self.

"Kinda far," he said frowning as he tried to guesstimate how far it could possibly be from where they were now.

"But we now have less than two hours to make zee dish!" cried Chef M.

"Oh, right," remembered Peter. "I know. We could act like its spring, and then maybe your blueberry bushes would be fooled into making blueberries."

"Ah, yes. That's subtle subterfuge," agreed Basil. "We could all pull out our spring outfits and put them on. I look simply smashing in pastels!" Puffing out his chest, he caught a glimpse of himself in one of the shiny pans hanging on the kitchen wall. He began to admire what he thought was a most beautiful reflection.

"Dude, that is soooooo dumb," said Marjoram rolling her eyes.

"Well I suppose you have a better idea?" he snapped.

"Yeah, I do. We could raid the Fricassee Fairy's Ice Cave. It's rumored she's hidden all sorts of berries next to her stash of stolen, golden pears. You know: raspberries, strawberries, gooseberries, boysenberries, blackberries, elderberries, cranberries and yes, big batches of ..." to which everyone shouted, "Blueberries!!!"

For a brief moment they thought about the Ice Cave. This was quickly followed by the mice wringing their paws, shaking their heads and generally looking quite worried.

"Is going there bad?" asked Peter, hoping of course they would say, "No."

"It's not so bad," answered Rosemary.

"If you don't mind certain death," said Marjoram dryly, shooting the other mice a glance.

Chef M shook his head. "Impossible! I cannot go to zee Ice Cave. Someone must stay here and prepare zee rest of zee meal."

"Fair 'nuf," said Marjoram. "We'll be back lickety-split."

Rosemary added, "I say we take Gothel with us, and dress warmly."

She flew over to an iron skillet hanging on the wall. Picking up a nearby spoon, she gave the skillet a good smack. Suddenly, a hidden panel in the wall drew back to reveal a cedar chest marked, "Winter Duds." The chest rolled out and its lid popped open to showcase a large array of cold weather outfits. Each piece of clothing floated up and found its way to the perfect owner. Belinda got cranberry colored mittens decorated with snowflakes, a matching hat, scarf and a vintage pair of bright yellow snow clogs. Peter's accessories came in pale blue and had penguins in the pattern. Basil, Marjoram and Rosemary each got mice-sized duds in cranberry, silver and pink, respectively. Plus, each mouse got a pair of fluffy, matching earmuffs that floated over and plopped onto their heads.

After the mice looked from one to the other, they lifted their chins toward the ceiling and yelled, "Gothel!"

A rumbling started, slowly at first. Then it turned to a banging, and then a tremor as the Royal Refrigerators began to shake wildly. The huge double doors to one of the Below Freezing refrigerators flew open. Inside it was Gothel, who had somehow managed to wedge himself in-between three of the refrigerator's shelves. He sort of resembled a lumpy green s. Head on the top shelf, belly in the middle and two clawed feet sticking out from either side of mustard, mayonnaise and pickle jars on the bottom shelf.

"Z'ere you are!" cried Chef M glaring sternly. He added, "What are you doing in my refrigerator?"

Gothel's cheeks were puffed out with something he was munching, which after a few quick chews, he managed to swallow. He then attempted to disentangle himself from great mounds of delicious-looking food. So wedged in was Gothel, that he had to start by sucking in his belly in order to have enough room to free his legs. No small task, since his tummy billowed out from all the snacking. After several attempts, he let out a *Burp!* so loud the pots and pans on the far wall rattled. Embarrassed, he covered his mouth with his claws and grinned sheepishly. Now a little less gassy, he could slide out with ease and was soon unwedged. He stood fully upright, all eight feet of him.

Even though Gothel was very big and very green, after seeing his goofy side, Peter and Belinda were no longer afraid. Not in the least.

"Do you always eat that way?" asked Belinda sweetly, charmed by the gargoyle's child-like manner.

"Gothel doesn't talk like the rest of us," Rosemary answered for him.

"But da dude sure can communicate," added Marjoram, winking at Gothel who winked back.

"Oh, my word, yes indeed," agreed Basil shaking his head.

"Gothel looks like he enjoys eating," observed Belinda.

"You got that right. And da dude's a crazy-cool vegetarian. Way into that organic stuff. Eats all day, but doesn't get fat," bragged Marjoram.

"Wow!" exclaimed Peter, thinking how much he would enjoy eating all day.

"Excusez-moi. I hate to interrupt but have you all forgotten we are under zee time pressure?" said Chef M sounding stressed.

"Oh, snap," exclaimed Marjoram "We gotta split! Everybody ready?" They nodded. "Good. Gothel, can you help us get to da Ice Cave?"

Gothel's eyes suddenly grew wide, as a guttural "Aaarrggrumph?" came out of his mouth.

"I know it's dangerous," answered Rosemary. "But Chef M's right. There's no time to waste. We have to go."

Gothel nodded and motioned them to follow him as Chef M called out, "Au revoir. Bon chance! Good luck!"

Gothel quickly led them to the opening of a dark tunnel at the furthest end of the kitchen. The entrance was low and framed by ancient beams. An old lantern hung from the top.

Gothel hit one of the beams right in the center with his claw. It popped forward to reveal a hidden drawer. From this drawer, Gothel grabbed a handful of candles and handed them out, keeping one for himself. He placed his candle inside the hanging lantern, and as he took it down, it lit up by itself. At the same time, everyone else's candles lit up.

"Whoa," cried Belinda, startled by the mysterious flames.

Shining his lantern to lead the way, Gothel started down a set of steep, wooden steps. They creaked dangerously. Everyone followed with caution, painfully aware that at any moment one of the old rotted boards could give way. The steps grew smaller and smaller as the staircase wound its way down.

The further they descended, the thicker and danker the air grew. Soon it became difficult to breathe. Lack of oxygen made everyone's candles grow dim and flicker, which made their surroundings dance with spooky shadows.

Without realizing how ridiculous it sounded, Peter blurted out, "Are we there yet?"

Everyone burst out laughing. Then he got it too, and joined them. They laughed so hard the mice had to stop and hug their bellies in order to not get serious side-aches. The tension had been broken. Now they could go on a little lighter and more confident than before.

Gothel's sharp pointy ears heard it first, a faint *drip* that reverberated. He knew they were getting closer.

On they went. It felt endless. The air grew steadily cooler and there was a slight breeze, which turned into wind. As they reached the bottom of the stairs, their candles all blew out. Grabbing each other's hands, paws, and claws they forged ahead, more slowly, of course. Luckily, Gothel had keen night vision.

No one dared speak as they shuffled along what felt like a slippery, cold surface. Before anyone had a chance to give it too much thought, a louder *DRIP* reverberated again. Only this time everyone heard it.

"Where are we?" whispered Peter choosing his question carefully this time.

"The Ice Cave. I think we're almost there," answered Rosemary.

Suddenly, a cold wind howled through them. With it came a faint, eerie blue glow. The temperature continued to drop as they went on. At the same time, the light grew steadily stronger, and finally they could see their surroundings. They had been walking on a floor of flat, wet rocks.

Directly before them was the entrance to a magnificent crystal cave. The closer they got, the colder the wind blew, and all but Gothel tightened their scarves. He didn't need one, for he came from an ancient line of cold-blooded gargoyles.

They approached the Ice Cave cautiously. The Fricassee Fairy might very well be lurking about. When the coast looked clear, Gothel motioned everyone to follow him in.

The first chamber they entered was filled with magnificent furniture made out of ice. Each piece glittered with a silvery blue glow. Deeper into the cavern, the frigid air caused their exhales to billow out like the puffs from a smoky dragon.

Soon they came upon a room filled with massive ice chests. Each chest had the name of its contents carved into the lid. As they passed, Basil read each one out loud. "Gold, silver, bronze, brass, tin. No, that's not what we're looking for," he commented. "Bread, cheese, butter, eggs." Then, "Sassafras, sasparilla, coriander, piccalilli. Piccalilli? No, that simply won't do," he said. The further they went, the more precious the contents became. "Rubies, diamonds, golden pears, blueberries, bananas. Oh dear, 'fraid not."

He was about to continue on when everyone shouted,

"BLUEBERRIES!"

Marjoram clicked into high gear with, "Sah-nap! Let's grab 'em and go." So they all hurried about the task. The chest they were after was on the very top of the tallest stack of chests. Gothel's long, powerful arms stretched up and jiggled the bottom chests just enough for the one he wanted to topple down. It landed with a loud, shattering crash. The top flew open to reveal a treasure-trove of the ripest, bluest berries.

Those who had pockets filled them. The others used their hats. When they had all taken as much as they could carry, they ran toward the cave's exit.

"Stop them!" echoed throughout the cave. "Thieves! They must be stopped!!" crackled the voice of the Fricassee Fairy.

Suddenly, something started oozing out of the walls. This gooey substance began transforming into an army of giant white spiders. Glistening like icicles, their long legs clicked as they descended the walls and hit the ground. Their frightening bodies were all covered with thick, white hair. But by far their most disturbing feature was a large, single eye directly above a row of three sharp, thorny mouths. They let out a series of piercing, blood-thirsty shrieks as they raced forward. Seeing this, the small band from Enchanted Thyme had no choice but to run with all their might.

With longer strides, Gothel reached the mouth of the Ice Cave before anyone else. He stood rigid in anticipation of their arrival. The mice were the first to pass through, followed closely behind by Peter who was huffing and puffing strongly. Turning to his sister, he found, to his horror, she wasn't there. In a total panic he yelled, "Belinda!!!" but she didn't answer.

Peter started back to look for her, but Gothel put out his arm to stop him and Rosemary said sharply, "Let Gothel go. You're no match for the Siberian Arachnids." Peter hesitated for a moment. This allowed Gothel just enough time to take off with super speed in the direction they had come from.

Belinda didn't seem to be anywhere. Not in the room with all the chests nor the one before it. Frantically, Gothel ran back and forth.

Finally, he spotted a tiny hand sticking out from under a gigantic piece of furniture. Running on the sheet of ice in her vintage yellow clogs had caused Belinda to slip and fall. She had landed hard on one knee and hit her head on the edge of one of the large, icy tables, her small limp body sliding down and landing underneath it. She was now completely sprawled out and not moving.

Gothel started toward her, but two Siberian Arachnids reached her first, their mouths *ta-click, ta-click, ta-clicking* while their hideous bodies bobbed and weaved as they hovered over their intended prey.

Regaining consciousness, Belinda tried to lift herself up, but when she saw the spiders above her, she screamed and fainted straightaway. They crouched lower on either side of her, their mouths *ta-click, ta-clicking* more rapidly.

Just as the spider's multiple mouths began to clamp down on Belinda's neck, a large green fist smashed into its soft underbelly. The spider went flying like a white shooting star with Belinda's cranberry scarf still clenched in its teeth. The other Siberian Arachnid spun around to face Gothel as it let out an ear- splitting *screeeeech*. It rushed toward him. In flashes of green and white colliding, they started to fight. Suddenly, the spider went flying in the same direction as the rest of the oncoming Arachnid army. It crashed into its own troops, scattering them here and there like bowling pins. This gave Gothel just enough time to scoop Belinda up and run back to where the others were waiting.

Gothel and Belinda had almost reached safety when one of the spiders gained on them and spit out a gooey substance. With amazing, split-second timing, Peter grabbed a small flat rock and held it up to deflect the awful string of goo. It hit and clung, turning the rock a sickly yellow-green and causing it to disintegrate. Falling, Peter knocked into Gothel and Belinda as all three fell past the boundaries of the Ice Cave. The Siberian Arachnids and their deadly projectile couldn't reach them now, for they had no powers outside of their cave.

"You didn't stop them! Fools!" screeched the Fricassee Fairy's voice. But it was too late.

Peter, Belinda and Gothel struggled to catch their breath. Now safe, though with a bump on her head and a badly skinned knee, Belinda managed a full grin as she gushed, "You saved my life!"

But just as she was about to tell Peter how proud of him she was, Rosemary exclaimed, "We have to hurry! There's hardly any time left!"

Everyone immediately jumped up. Gothel cradled Belinda in his arms and they made their way back over the flat slippery rocks, up the rickety spiral staircase, and finally ... to the Royal Kitchen.

Chef M was frantically pacing back and forth, shaking his head and exclaiming, "Oooh-la-la-la-la! Where are zay?" Just as the track he had been wearing in the floor started to become knee deep, Gothel and Belinda burst through the door, followed by the others.

Chef M raced toward them with open arms. He hugged each of them so forcefully that they almost passed out. "I am most happy to zee you!!" he exclaimed and again squeezed them with another bear hug.

"Careful!" cried Belinda, "We're full of ripe blueberries."

The Fricassee Fairy's
Siberian Ice Pops

Makes 10 ice pops

2 lbs. peeled, seeded and diced honeydew melon

1/4 cup fresh lemon juice

2/3 cup sugar

2 Tablespoons light corn syrup

1 cup fresh blueberries

- Place honeydew melon in a food processor with lemon juice and puree until smooth.

- Add sugar and corn syrup.

- Pulse until combined.

- Pour into a fine sieve or strainer placed over a large bowl.

- Using the back of a ladle or large spoon, stir and push the liquid mixture through the sieve and into the bowl. Discard any solids left in the sieve.

- Stir blueberries into melon mixture.
- Divide into ten, 4oz. ice pop molds.
- Freeze overnight.

~ Note ~

- If you don't have ice pop molds, don't worry. Be creative! Try using small paper cups with Popsicle sticks or several ice cube trays with plastic drinking straws that have been cut into two inch pieces.

- Either way, freeze the mixture in the cups or trays for two hours and then push the Popsicle sticks or straws into the partially frozen treat. Continue freezing.

"DIABOLICALLY GOOD!"
CACKLED THE FRICASSEE FAIRY.

Chapter Fourteen

A pain in the buttocks can be a great motivator, especially when that pain is attached to a set of razor-sharp teeth. Up shot Orgoglio from where he and Creepy had landed! Straight out behind him was Creepy, holding on with a vice-like grip.

Orgoglio began to run, hoping the movement might weaken Creepy's jaws and cause him to fall. Hobbling with a very sore, but unbroken ankle, Orgoglio picked up speed. He tried to reach back and grab the offending reptile, but the monster's awkward placement made this incredibly difficult. What to do? What to do?!!

Then Orgoglio spotted a tree trunk split in half and still smoldering from one of the Fricassee Fairy's lightening bolts. "Yes, indeedy. That will do quite nicely," thought Orgoglio, who was more than anxious to put an end to this unfortunate turn of events.

Orgoglio ran up to the still-burning embers. Creepy was, of course, close behind. The giant, butt smarting, turned to sit on the red-hot coals with Creepy making the perfect cushion between him and the dying fire. The embers hissed as they burned into the monster's skin. He let go just as Orgoglio stood up again.

Suffice it to say, the damage to this monster-beast was just enough to convince him to beat a hasty retreat. He slinked back into the cool ooze of the nearby swamp, ready to tend his wounds and his wounded pride. Orgoglio had won this round, but it would be far from the last.

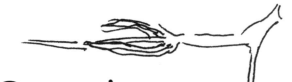

Creepy's
Behind~the~Fall
Frappé

Serves 2

1 ripe banana, peeled and broken into pieces

1 cup fresh or frozen strawberries

1/2 cup blueberries

1/2 cup non~fat plain or berry~flavored yogurt

1/2 cup apple juice

(Add six ice cubes if you do not use frozen

strawberries.)

- Place all ingredients in a blender. Blend on high
  speed for 20-30 seconds or until smooth.

- Pour into glasses and enjoy.

"MMMMMM." CREEPY SAYS IT'S SOOTHING.

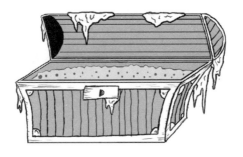

Chapter Fifteen

*A*aah!" sighed Chef M as Peter and Belinda put the finishing touches on a dish they felt royally befitted Queen Topstead. Peter stirred the oats while Belinda added the honey. They all finished by topping it with mounds of plump blueberries. Just in the nick of time, too.

For at exactly six o'clock, her loyal manservant, Withers, arrived. "Her Majesty wishes to dine in the South Wing," he announced grandly.

"Voilà!" Chef M motioned toward the masterpiece as he grinned at Peter, Belinda, Gothel and the mice. "This should do zee trick." Bowing, he proudly placed the dish on a tray and handed it over. As soon as Withers whisked the dish away, their initial merriment grew into downright exaltation.

Meanwhile, in the South Wing, Queen Topstead anxiously

awaited her royal supper. She grew more irritated with each passing grain of sand that fell through her hourglass. Fearing another one of her explosive outbursts, the servants began shrinking in stature, wishing they could become the size of ants and disappear altogether.

Just then, Withers appeared at the door with the tray that held a covered dish and a silver spoon. As he lifted the lid, Queen Topstead's eyes grew wide as saucers. Her mouth watered as she pounced on the silver spoon and began digging into the mound of blue splendor. When the spoon proved far too small, she plunged in with both hands, purple juice splattering everywhere and running down her chin.

Back in the kitchen, a bell on the wall began to ring. Tinkling faintly at first, it grew stronger. Everyone stopped talking and froze.

Then Chef M broke the silence. "Ah zee Queen, she wishes to let us know …," but before he could finish, another bell rang. "Ah, now zat bell means zee Queen is pretty happy weez her meal. If zee third bell rings, ah, success! She is satisfied and we are victorious. *Brrrriiiing!* "Bravo! C'est magnifique!" shouted Chef M as they all started to cheer. But then, a fourth bell began to ring. *Brrrriiiing! Brrrrriiiiiiiiiing!* Their cheering came to a halt. *Brriiiiiiiiiiiiiiiiiiiiiiiiiiiiiiiiiiiiiiiiiiing!*

Startled, Peter looked around to find himself not in Enchanted Thyme, but in a strange place. He was in some sort of cocoon. It was blue and kind of fluffy, not unpleasant. What was that thing next to him? A table? ... with a lamp?!

This was definitely not Enchanted Thyme. It was … *Briiing* … his own bedroom.

The bell continued its loud irritating ringing until Belinda stumbled over and shut off the alarm. She looked at her brother still in bed. "Peter?" she asked hesitantly.

"Yeah?" he answered slowly.

"Where are we?" asked Belinda.

"Our house, I guess … why?" he answered stiffly, really not sure where he was.

"Nothing," she said stretching her arms up in order to wake up more fully.

"Strange dreams," she said groggily.

"You too? Really? Me too!! A crazy place."

Curiously, Belinda said, "Yeah. With a giant."

"An evil fairy?"

"And a Queen!" they said together.

But before Peter could elaborate, Dad's familiar voice called up from downstairs, "Time to get up. You two sleepyheads getting up?"

"Sure Dad," they answered almost in unison.

"All right," he continued, "it's almost seven thirty. Please hurry and get in the shower. I made you my famous granola. With lots of fresh, juicy blueberries. C'mon, it's ready."

Peter and Belinda looked at each other for a moment in disbelief.

"Dreams are weird, but not real," said Peter, half sounding like he was trying to convince himself.

Belinda added, "Oh, sure. Everybody knows that. Now c'mon. We'd better get going."

As she grabbed the school clothes she had set out the night before and turned toward the bathroom, she felt something small but heavy weighing down her pajama pocket. So she reached in to see what it was. And as she turned back to Peter to remind him that it was her turn to shower first, she pulled out a small, shiny object and held it out in front of her. Opening her hand, she saw it was a tiny, golden pear.

Gasping in amazement, they heard what sounded like a faint, far-away voice. It seemed to be coming from the book on their night table.

The voice whispered, "I'm not done with you." It grew louder. "Trying to outsmart me? HAH! Think you can save the Queendom? Ha,ha,ha,ha,hee,hee,heeeeeee!" cackled the Fricassee Fairy as the book began to glow red. Then the book ceased and all was silent.

After a moment, Belinda asked, "Should we? I mean, if the mice need us?"

"Can we?" Peter replied.

"Sure!" they both agreed.

"Besides, Orgoglio might be in trouble." cried Belinda.

"And Gothel."

"And Chef Michelle Mon Shoo Chablis Poo Boo."

"The Queen, too."

They both smiled. And with that, their decision was made. When the time came, they would gladly go back to help their friends in Enchanted Thyme.

"And you know what's even more terrible?" Peter asked with a look of great concern.

"What?"

"No one ever bothered to explain to me what 'Farklemped' means."

"Oh, yeah," nodded Belinda. Their voices trailed off as they made their way out of their room and into the hall.

And so it was, the end of this adventure ... for now.

FINI

The Ultimate
Homemade
Granola
with
Fresh Blueberries

Yields about 8 cups

1 ½ cups quick-rolled oats, uncooked

2 cups unfrosted mini-wheat cereal or bran flakes

1 cup sunflower seeds

1½ cups dried cranberries

3/4 cup yellow golden raisins

1/2 cup sliced almonds

1/2 cup flaked coconut

1/2 cup carob chips

1/2 cup vegetable oil

1/2 cup honey

1 Tablespoon molasses

1 teaspoon vanilla extract

Parchment paper

1/4 cup blueberries for each serving

- Preheat oven to 350.
- Place oats, cereal, sunflower seeds, cranberries, raisins, almonds, coconut and carob in a large mixing bowl.
- Toss gently trying not to break up the cereal.
- Place oil, honey, molasses and vanilla in a saucepan.
- Bring to a simmer, mixing over medium heat until combined.
- Pour honey mixture over granola and toss with a metal spoon. (Be careful not to burn yourself.)
- Spread granola onto a parchment-lined baking pan.
- Bake 15-20 minutes until golden brown.
- Let cool to room temperature.
- Store in air-tight container.

WHEN READY TO EAT, SPRINKLE WITH FRESH BLUEBERRIES. YOU CAN ENJOY THIS RECIPE AS A SNACK, A BREAKFAST CEREAL, OR ANYTIME YOU HAVE A ROYAL HUNGER. IT IS, AFTER ALL, A DISH FIT FOR A QUEEN.

Glossary

Adjective: (ad·jek·tive) (This word is a noun.)
A word that describes a person, place or thing
(Example:) The green jacket got a lot of notice. ("Green" is the adjective that describes the jacket.)

Adverb: (ad·verb) (This word is a noun.)
A descriptive word the is used to modify a verb, adjective or even a whole sentence. It usually ends with "ly"
(Example: 1) Frank turned around slowly. (slowly is the adverb that modifies turned around.)
(Example: 2) The window is slightly dirty. (slightly is the adverb that modifies dirty.)
(Example: 3) Loudly, Beth made the announcement. (loudly is the adverb that modifies the whole sentence.)

Affront: (a·front) (This word is a noun.)
1) As a noun it means an insult
(Example:) Not expecting such a rude and uncalled for affront to his behind, Basil let out a very loud "squeeeek!"

Agitation: (ag·i·ta·shun) (This word is a noun.)
1) A very nervous or uncomfortable feeling
2) Something someone does or says to get people all excited or riled up to either support or fight something
3) A very strong shaking or stirring of something (usually a liquid)
(Example: 1) Chef M paced back and forth with great agitation.
(Example: 2) Her agitation of the crowd got them to demand new schoolbooks.
(Example: 3) Billy opened the lid of the washing machine to watch the agitation of the water inside.

Aplomb: (a·plom) (This word is a noun.)
Showing great confidence, gracefulness or skill, especially in stressful situations
(Example:) Rosemary gently pushed Belinda toward the Queen and whispered, "Bow and curtsy." Even frightened, Belinda was able to do this with beautiful aplomb.

Apparition: (ap·pa·ri·shun) (This word is a noun.)
The appearance of something unusual such as a person or thing that you didn't expect; or something ghostly like … a ghost
(Example:) Rosemary noticed the dark apparition that had begun to follow them.

Arachnids: (a·rak·nidz) (This word is a plural noun. The singular form is Arachnid.)
Wingless animals that have eight limbs (could be legs or pinchers) and no antennae. This includes Spiders, Scorpions, Mites and some other critters
(Example:) The Siberian Arachnids and their deadly projectiles couldn't reach them now, for they had no powers outside of their cave.

Beacon: (bee·kun) (This word is a noun.)
1) A light, fire or even a radio signal that is used as a signal to help guide the way toward or away from something, the way a signal fire leads rescuers to find people stranded on a deserted island

2) A person or thing that gives inspiration or guidance to others
(Example: 1) We followed your beacon and it lead us right to you.
(Example: 2) "Tell me it was successful. Be the beacon of light in my presently dreary existence."

Billowed: (bil·low·d) (This word is a verb. It is the past-tense form of billow.)
1) To fill up with air or to make something swell up
2) To float through the air like a cloud
(Example: 1) His tummy billowed out from all the snacking.
(Example: 2) The smoke from our campfire billowed up into the air.

Blathering: (bla·ther·ring) (This word can either be a noun or a verb.)
1) As a noun this words means silly, or dumb talk that just seems to go on and on.
2) As a verb it means to talk in a in a silly, nonsensical or unintelligent way.
(Example: 1) Ignoring this blathering, Belinda slowly tiptoed toward the bookshelf.
(Example: 2) While trying to think of the answer, Bob just kept blathering on and on.

Bulbous: (bul·bus) (This word is an adjective.)
1) Big round and swollen looking
2) Something that grows out of a plant bulb (most likely a plant)
(Example: 1) The shutters flew open and nothing but a large, bulbous nose poked through.
(Example: 2) The Lilly is a bulbous plant.

Catapulted: (kat·uh·pult·ed) (This word is a verb. It is the past tense of catapult.)
This word means to be thrown through the air with great force
(Example:) The book opened and three furry orbs catapulted out of it.
(note: in the present tense, the word catapult can also be a noun. It is a large machine that throws things.)

Cloaked: (kloke·d) (This word is an adjective.)
Anything that is hidden, concealed, covered or even blanketed
(Example:) It was a forest cloaked in eerie silence.

Cold-blooded: (kold·blood·ed) (This word is an adjective.)
1) An animal whose body temperature can change based on the temperature of the area that it is in, usually fish or reptiles Mammals (like humans for example) can't do this.
(Example:) He came from an ancient line of cold-blooded gargoyles.

Colossal: (ko·loss·al) (This word is an adjective.)
1) Something unusually large
2) Something that makes an unusually strong impression
(Example: 1) The Empire State Building is a colossal structure.
(Example: 2)"What a colossal bully!" she exclaimed as she stood on the tip of her pointe shoes.

Commodities: (kom·od·it·eez) (This word is a plural noun. The singular noun is commodity.)
1) Anything that can be bought or sold
2) Anything that people value
(Example: 1) Gold and silver are valuable commodities.
(Example: 2) Peter and Belinda were also lucky to have the coolest in status symbol commodities; a chef for a parent.

Composure: (kom·po·sure) (This word is a noun.)
Self control; staying calm cool and collected when things get scary or crazy
(Example:) "Yeah?" said Peter trying to regain his composure.

Cyclops: (sy·klops) (This word is a noun.)
A make-believe being that only has one eye in the middle of it's forehead
(Example:) He was always up for reading about a good adventure, but
not necessarily going on one; especially one that might involve strange
creatures, or far away lands, or scary monsters, or dark woods, or evil
stepsisters, or flesh-eating Cyclops, or two headed beasts.

Demeanor: (dee·meen·er) (This word is a noun.)
How somebody or something behaves or looks like they behave
(Example:) Despite her delicate Ballerina demeanor, she could pack a wallop.

Descendants: (dee·send·ents) (This word is a plural noun. The singular
noun is descendant)
1) The offspring (sometimes distant) of people, animals or plants that were
born before them
2) Objects whose design was based on something that has been made
before
(Example: 1) They're descendants of a very famous chef.
(Example: 2) These fountains are the descendants of the ones used in
ancient Rome.

Discourse: (dis·korss) (This word is a noun.)
A very long speech, discussion or debate about a subject
(Example:) I see you managed to choose a book without the usual discourse.

Disentangle: (diss·en·tan·gle) (This word is a verb.)
1) To unravel things that are all knotted or twisted together
2) Getting yourself out of a conversation, position or situation that you
don't want to be in
(Example: 1) In order to use the rope, Tom first had to disentangle it from
the other ropes.
(Example: 2) He attempted to disentangle himself from great mounds of
delicious food.

Dust ruffle: (dust·ruffle) (This word is a noun.)
A long piece of fabric that runs around the entire edge of a bed and goes to
the floor, in order to keep dust from collecting under the mattress
(Example:) Her wings tangled in the dust ruffle and "*Ker-plonk*," she landed
ungracefully in a heap on the floor.

Embers: (em·bers) (This word is a plural noun. The Singular noun is ember.)
Small glowing objects (usually wood or charcoal) left over after a fire has
gone out
(Example:) His eyes glow like embers in the dark.

Emphatically: (em·fat·ick·ly) (This word is an adverb.)
Something that is done with a lot of enthusiasm, energy or importance
(Example:) "Certainly not," replied Basil emphatically.

Enthralled: (en·thrawll·d) (This word is an adjective.)
To be totally fascinated, amazed and filled with delight
(Example:) Our two were so enthralled that they scarcely noticed the mice
flying them in circles above the book like a pair of jumbo jets.

Exaltation: (ex·all·tā·shun) (This word is a noun.)
An intense feeling of extreme joy or elation
(Example:) After the Queen's manservant whisked away her food, their initial merriment soon grew into downright exaltation.

Exhilarating: (ex·ill·er·ate·ing) (This word is an adjective.)
Something that makes you feel energized, very happy or very cheerful
(Example:) There's always that moment of reckless abandon. The decision, followed by a plunge. Then all of a sudden you're in an unfamiliar world; murky, muffled, yet totally exhilarating.

Farklempt: (fer·klempt) (This word is an adjective.)
The feeling someone gets when they don't know what to do about a situation and are all choked up
(Example) "Yeah, everyone here is fresh outta any clue," added Marjoram. "Farklempt?" asked the Magic Mushroom.

Fathom: (fa·thum) (This word could be a noun or a verb.)
1) As a verb it means to understand something that is normally very confusing or important.
2) As a noun it is a unit of measurement used to tell how deep water is.
(Example: 1) She was trying not to fathom what a horrible fate would await them if they were caught by the Fricassee Fairy.
(Example: 2) The submarine went down 50 fathoms into the ocean.

Feeble: (fee·bull) (This word is an adjective.)
1) Physically or mentally weak
2) A very unlikely (usually not true) excuse that people find very hard to believe
(Example: 1) It was hard for the feeble old man to get around.
(Example: 2) As he continued to speak all eyes bore into him and his feeble excuse.

Festered: (fess·terd) (This word is a verb past tense. The present tense is fester.)
1) Something that has been left to decay and rot (often because of an infection that has gone untreated
2) To have let bad feelings build up inside until they become terrible thoughts
(Example: 1) He went to the doctor because he didn't want his wound to fester.
(Example: 2) Her anger had festered over the years and caused her to become quite a hideous being.

Flourish: (floor·ish) (This word can be either a verb or a noun.)
1) As a verb is means to grow and continue growing healthy and strong.
2) It also means to wave something in a very big showy way.
3) As a noun it means a big body movement (like a wide wave of the hand) that is meant to get attention.
4) It is also a design at the beginning or end of a piece of writing to add decoration to it.
(Example: 1) The plant continued to flourish in the greenhouse.
(Example: 2) Both guards bowed with a flourish.
(Example: 3) With a flourish, the host announced the arrival of the guest of honor.
(Example: 4) The sentence began and ended with a flourish.

Folly: (foll·ee) (This word is a noun.)
1) To act in a silly or foolish way
2) A big project that will in the end cost a lot more money and time than it was worth
(Example: 1) Our Queen, though once jolly, is consumed by dark folly. But we're told you might bring her good cheer.
(Example: 2) Building that nuclear powered, twenty-five foot flying jelly jar was pure folly.

Frenetic: (fren·et·ick) (This word is an adjective.)
Acting frantic, frenzied or very, very active
(Example:) Now our dancing giant moved from Mexican rhythms to a more frenetic Salsa.

Furtive: (fur·tiv) (This word is an adjective.)
Done in a way that is not meant to be noticed
(Example:) After a small furtive sigh, he continued.

Futile: (fu·tile) or (fu·tull) (This word is an adjective.)
Useless
(Example:) His first attempt was futile.

Gargantuan: (gar·gan·chew·an) (This word is an adjective.)
Really huge in size or in number
(Example:) Their gargantuan army was not far behind.

Ghastly: (gas·tly) (This word is an adjective.)
Frightening, ugly, shocking, horrifying or bad
(Example:) There seemed to be a great number of stories about the Fricassee Fairy, each one more ghastly than the last.

Groovy: (groo·vy) (This word is an adjective.)
An old expression that describes someone or something that is more attractive, excellent or better than most of their kind
(Example:) "These walls are psychedelic tie-dye! Too groovy!" she exclaimed.

Guesstimate: (gess·tim·ate) (This word is a verb.)
To estimate or assume a value without all of the necessary information
(Example:) He tried to guesstimate how far it could possibly be from where they were now.

Guffaws: (guff·aws) (This word is a plural noun. The singular noun is guffaw.)
Very loud wild laughs
(Example:) But just as the mice's tittering squeaks grew more frequent, they began turning into deep guffaws.

Hedge fund: (hedge·fund) (This word is a noun.)
A company that invests money in very risky ways in order to make a lot more money back
(Example:) Father runs a hedge fund and Mother stays home to take care of us.

Hideous: (hid·ee·us) (This word is an adjective.)
Horribly ugly or scary
(Example:) Gothel started toward her, but two Siberian Arachnids reached her first, their mouths *ta-click, ta-click, ta-clicking* while their hideous bodies bobbed and weaved.

Hellions: (hell·ee·yuns) (This word is a plural noun. The singular noun

is hellion.)
A rowdy person or a troublemaker
(Example:) Those boys always disrupt the class. They sure are hellions.
Humongous: (hyoo·mun·gus) (This word is an adjective.)
Very very large
(Example:) A family of humongous beetles scuttled right in front of Peter.
Illuminated: (ill·oo·min·ate·ed) (This word is a verb. It is the past tense version of illuminate.)
1) To light up a thing or an area
2) To make something (especially somebody's face) look happy
3) To explain something's and make it understandable
4) To decorate something with lights or other bright things
(Example 1:)Each step they took illuminated a new mushroom.
(Example 2:)Betty's smile illuminated her face.
(Example 3:) Using the word in a sentence illuminated it's meaning.
(Example 4:)They Illuminated their house with holiday decorations.
Impenetrable: (im·pen·it·re·bull) (This word is an adjective.)
Something that cannot be passed through or gotten into
(Example:) Belinda rushed over to strike an impenetrable stance in front of the bookshelf.
Incredulously: (in·crej·yoo·luss·ly) (This word is an adverb.)
A skeptical or disbelieving way
(Example:) "No, nanny does that." answered Jennifer incredulously as she continued to stare out the school bus window.
Indubitably: (in·doo·pid·abe·ly) (This word is an adjective.)
Totally true and without a doubt
(Example:) She'll be satisfied. Am I right?" She turned to the mice. "Absolutely." beamed Rosemary. "Indubitably," added Basil. "Cool beans." quipped Marjoram giving Belinda and a reluctant Peter, a high five.
Instantly: (in·stant·ly) (This word is an adverb.)
Something that happens immediately
(Example:) Instantly, Basil regained his composure.
Interminable: (in·ter·min·able) (This word is an adjective.)
So long or so boring it seems to take forever
(Example:) It was an interminable split second before Peter was able to get out a "Shhhhhh" while still not moving a muscle.
Invincible: (in·vin·sib·le) (This word is an adjective.)
Can't be defeated
(Example:) In her mind, she was an invincible giant.
Iridescent: (ear·id·ess·ent) (This word is an adjective.)
Shiny, bright or colorful
(Example:) The turban had an iridescent blue gem smack in the middle of it.
Lumbering: (lum·ber·ing) (This word is an adjective.)
Moving slowly, heavily or clumsily
(Example:) These moves were all quite graceful for a big hearted but lumbering giant.
Magenta: (maj·ent·uh) (This word is an adjective.)
A bright purplish-pink color

(Example:) These officious visions in purple were stationed on either side of a drawbridge. Frowning under ridiculously tall, magenta-colored hats.

Mayhem: (may·hem) (This word is a noun.)
Total chaos and craziness
(Example:) This jolly mayhem continued around and around the room, better than any amusement park ride they'd ever taken.

Mellifluous: (mell·i·floo·us) (This word is an adjective.)
Something that is soothing and nice to listen to
(Example:) "Delighted," glowed Basil, always more than happy to show off his mellifluous voice.

Militaristic: (mill·tar·iss·tik) (This word is an adjective.)
Believing in or living by a military code of conduct and behavior
(Example:) These militaristic visions in purple were stationed on either side of a drawbridge.

Molten: (mole·ten) (This word is an adjective.)
Melted, usually due to heat
(Example:) Thinking about this made his body feel heavy and molten.

Mt. Rushmore: (mount· rush·more) (This word is a noun.)
A mountain in South Dakota that has the faces of George Washington, Abraham Lincoln, Thomas Jefferson and Theodore Roosevelt carved into it
(Example:) "Yeeeeeeaaah!" shouted Peter as he took a giant leap off the bed right into the pile of pillows he proudly dubbed Mt. Rushmore.

Noun: (nown) (This word is a noun.)
Any person, place or thing
(Example:) Billy has a nice house. (In this sentence Billy is a noun and so is house.

Novelty: (nov·el·tee) (This word is a noun.)
1) Something that is unusual and exciting or interesting (usually just for a short time)
2) A small inexpensive ornament or toy
(Example 1:) As this novelty began to wear off, they were left silently following the mice .
(Example 2:) The necklace made of shells was a cute little novelty.

Numerous: (noom·er·us) (This word is an adjective.)
In large numbers
(Example:) Peter and Belinda had thoughts too numerous to mention.

Orbs: (orbs) (This word is a plural noun. The singular noun is Orb.)
An object shaped like a ball
(Example:) Three furry orbs catapulted out of the book.

Papier mâché: (paper·mash·ay) (This word is a noun.)
A combination of paper strips and glue or plaster that is shaped when wet and dries into a hard object
(Example:) I'm making a volcano with papier maché and baking soda.

Peevishly: (pee·vish·ly) (This word is an adverb.)
Annoyed or in a bad mood
(Example:) "You already said that," pointed out Belinda peevishly.

Pointe shoes: (point·shooz) (This word is a plural noun. The singular

noun is Pointe Shoe.)
A special kind of shoes used for ballet dancing
(Example:) She won a scholarship to the Mousery Ballet School and hasn't taken off her pointe shoes or her tutu since.

Ponder: (pon·der) (This word is a verb.)
To think about something very deeply
(Example:) Peter stayed a few steps behind to ponder the situation.

Projectiles: (pro·jekt·iles) (This word is a plural noun. The singular noun is projectile.)
Objects that are thrown or launched with great force
(Example:) Their deadly projectiles couldn't reach them now.

Pronoun: (pro·nown) (This word is a noun.)
Any word that takes the place of a specific noun to make it more general
(Example:) Tommy walked to his friend's house. (In this sentence the word *his* is the pronoun.)

Protruding: (pro·troo·ding) (This word is an adjective.)
Something is sticking out
(Example:) He plunged his teeth into the nearest protruding part of the giant; his buttocks.

Psychedelic: (sy·ked·el·ik) (This word is an adjective.)
Wildly distorted or colorful
(Example:) "These walls are psychedelic tie-dye! Too groovy!"

Quipped: (kwippt) (This word is a past tense verb. The present tense is Quip.)
A cute, clever, sarcastic or funny comment that was made by someone
(Example:) Wait 'till you get a load a' Creepy," quipped Marjoram.

Rant: (rant) (This word is a noun.)
An angry, overly expressive, and sometimes violent way of speaking or writing
(Example:) As the final syllable in her rant finished, Rosemary whispered to Peter and Belinda, "The Queen's a bit grumpy today."

Reluctance: (re·luk·tense) (This word is a noun.)
A hesitance or even an unwillingness to do something
(Example:) Only with great reluctance did they continue on.

Remnant: (rem·nant) (This word is a noun.)
What has been cut off or left over from a larger thing, situation or time
(Example:) The pool was a sad remnant from when the fairy was still happy and in Queen Topstead's good graces.

Renegade: (ren·eh·gade) (This word is a noun.)
Someone or something that goes against or completely ignores normal everyday acceptable behavior
(Example:) They preferred to see themselves as renegade rodents with unflappable logic and penetrating insights.

Reptilian: (rep·till·yan) (This word is an adjective.)
Having at least some of the physical characteristics or behaviors of a lizard
(Example:) Creepy's reptilian head rose up from his long neck and remained deadly still.

Rollicking: (rol·lick·ing) (This word is an adjective.)
Something that is carefree, loud, energized and even wild (in a good way)

(Example:) Later that night, during a rollicking game of "bed & bounce," their Dad, Michael, called from downstairs

Savory: (save·or·ee) (This word is an adjective.)
1) A saltier or sharper flavor instead of a sweet one
2) Smelling or tasting delicious
(Example 1:)"Try one," encouraged Marjoram. "They're savory, not sweet."
(Example 2:) The meal I made for the party was quite savory, if I do say so myself.

Scarcely: (scare·slee) (This word is an adverb.)
Just barely, almost not at all or even in some cases totally not
(Example:) Our two were so enthralled that they scarcely noticed the mice circling them above the book like a pair of jumbo jets.

Semblance: (sem·blans) (This word is a noun.)
1) An imitation, copy or reproduction of something
2) A tiny amount of something.
(Example 1:)She leaned in closer, dropping any semblance of a smile, "I'm not only hungry, but voracious. See you then."
(Example 2:)Tony showed only the smallest semblance of interest in cleaning his room.

Singeing: (sinj·ing) (This word is a verb.)
The act of burning something slightly; not too badly but enough to remove any hair or feathers
(Example:) A bolt of fiery lightening flew past them singeing the delicate hair on Basil's left ear.

Skepticism: (skep·ti·sism) (This word is a noun.)
A doubt or reluctance to believe something that someone else believes to be true
(Example:) Despite his initial skepticism, he began enjoying himself.

Sojourn: (so·jern) (This word is a noun.)
A journey or a temporary visit
(Example:) "Back from your sojourn I see." She said sternly before breaking into a wide smile.

Soufflé: (soo·flay) (This word is a noun.)
A very light airy food that is baked or chilled. It is made especially light by using beaten or whisked eggs
(Example:) "Oh, Mon dieu!" the chef exclaimed as he spun around to face them. "My Soufflé! She will be ruined!"

Sous-chef: (soo·shef) (This word is a noun.)
The assistant to the main or head chef
(Example:) She motioned toward Peter and Belinda, "Chef M, I present you; two new sous-chefs.

Sovereign: (sov·er·in) (This word can be a noun or an adjective.)
1) As a noun this is a leader such as a Queen or an Emperor.
2) Also as a noun it is a gold coin that used to be used as money in England between the 1600's and the early 1900's.
3) As an adjective this word describes a person or place that is not ruled or controlled by any other place or person.
(Example 1:)"Yes, your Majesty. Certainly, dear Sovereign. Absolutely, your Grace," they repeated.

(Example 2:)The magical lamp was bought for only a soverign.
(Example 3:) The United States of America is a soverign nation.

Squinched: (skwinched) (This word is a past tense verb. The present these verb is squinch.)
1) The act of squeezing up your eyes or face
2) Crouching in order to seem smaller or fit into a small space
(Example 1:) "Ssshhhh," the mice warned with squinched looks on their faces.
(Example 2:) Mary squinched into the small crawl-space during the hide and seek game.

Strenuous: (stren·yoo·us) (This word is an adjective.)
Physically hard, tiring or draining
(Example:) Peter copied her and soon all their strenuous jungle gym days seemed to pay off.

Subterfuge: (sub·ter·fyooj) (This word is a noun.)
Something someone does to take attention away from something they don't want someone else to see or hear, a distraction
(Example:) "Ah, yes. That's subtle subterfuge," agreed Basil.

Suffice: (suff·ice) (This word is a verb.)
Enough to satisfy a need or explanation
(Example:) Suffice it to say, the damage to this monster beast was just enough to convince him to beat a hasty retreat.

Sullen: (sull·en) (This word is an adjective.)
1) A sad or bad attitude or a refusal to be social.
2) Gloomy because of gray, foggy or cloudy weather
(Example 1:) Breaking the brief sullen silence, Belinda exclaimed, "Hey! I've got an idea. Let's think-tank this problem."
(Example 2:) No one was out playing on this cold, sullen day.

Tangent: (tan·jent) (This word is a noun.)
1) A thought or action that suddenly turns to a totally different thought or action
2) A math term for a line or plane that touches (but doesn't cross) a surface or curve at only one point
(Example 1:) But before she could go off on another tangent, she caught herself and instead asked, "Tell me why you've decided to come here."
(Example 2:) In math class, Tom had to draw the tangent that touched the edge of the oval.

Thyme: (time) (This word is a noun.)
A plant whose little leaves are used either dried or fresh as a flavoring in cooking
(Example:) The chef added some fresh thyme to the stew she was making.

Toadstools: (tode·stoolz) (This word is a plural noun. The singular noun is toadstool.)
A poisonous kind of mushroom shaped like an umbrella In fairy-tales they is sometimes described as being red with white polka dots but in real life they aren't.
(Example:)These weren't umbrellas at all, they were giant mushrooms. Toadstools, to be exact.

Topsy-turvy: (topsy·turvy) (This word is an adjective.)
Turned upside-down, inside-out or any other confused, crazy way
(Example:) Everyone's topsy-turvy trying to figure out which recipe will
work, but so far no one has succeeded.

Tremendous: (tre·mend·us) (This word is an adjective.)
Very very huge, powerful, or impressive
(Example:) That beastyis a good eighty-six feet long, inky and shiny, with
blue-black scales and tremendous claws.

Unflappable: (un·flap·able) (This word is an adjective.)
Able to stay calm, cool and collected even in the worst circumstances
(Example:) They preferred to see themselves as renegade rodents with
unflappable logic.

Valiantly: (val·yent·ly) (This word is an adverb.)
Very very brave way that someone or something solved a problem or came to
the rescue of another person or thing
(Example:) This small detail didn't matter when it came to valiantly
protecting her friends.

Verb: (verb) (This word is a noun.)
1) Any action that someone or something is doing no matter how small or
large
2) The current condition of a person or thing
(Example 1:) Tony tried to move the huge stone. The word *move* is the verb.
(Example 2:) Nancy is cold. The word *is* is the verb.

Vintage: (vin·tij) (This word is an adjective.)
Something that is from an earlier time but is still in good condition
(Example:) Belinda got cranberry colored mittens decorated with
snowflakes, a matching hat, scarf and vintage pair of bright yellow snow
clogs.

Voracious: (vor·ay·shus) (This word is an adjective.)
1) Desperately wanting, needing or very quickly eating large amounts of
food
2) Unusually excited about doing an activity
(Example 1:) "I'm not only hungry, but voracious."
(Example 2:) Stuart is a voracious reader.

Wince: (winss) (This word can be either a verb or a noun.)
1) As a verb is means to make a facial expression or movement as a reaction
to fear, pain or the threat of fear or pain.
2) As a noun it is the expression or movement that someone or something
makes as a reaction to fear, pain or the threat of fear or pain.
(Example 1:)After getting her boot size and zipping them up, she noticed
Dad's slight wince of disapproval.
(Example 2:)Her wince was the result of the teachers announcement that
there will be a pop quiz.